AFTER-PARTY CONSEQUENCES

HEIDI RICE

PRESENTS

Harlequin®
PRESENTS™

ISBN-13: 978-1-335-93926-5

After-Party Consequences

 Harlequin Enterprises ULC
22 Adelaide St. West, 41st Floor
Toronto, Ontario M5H 4E3, Canada
www.Harlequin.com

Printed in Lithuania

Recycling programs for this product may not exist in your area.

MIX
Paper | Supporting responsible forestry
FSC® C021394

USA TODAY bestselling author **Heidi Rice** lives in London, England. She is married with two teenage sons—which gives her rather too much of an insight into the male psyche—and also works as a film journalist. She adores her job, which involves getting swept up in a world of high emotions; sensual excitement; funny, feisty women; sexy, tortured men; and glamorous locations where laundry doesn't exist. Once she turns off her computer, she often does chores—usually involving laundry!

Books by Heidi Rice

Harlequin Presents

Revealing Her Best Kept Secret
Stolen for His Desert Throne
Redeemed by My Forbidden Housekeeper
Hidden Heir with His Housekeeper
Revenge in Paradise

Passionately Ever After...

A Baby to Tame the Wolfe

Billion-Dollar Christmas Confessions

Unwrapping His New York Innocent

Hot Winter Escapes

Undoing His Innocent Enemy

Visit the Author Profile page
at Harlequin.com for more titles.

To Lucy and Nat! I had so much fun working on our fabulous stories, let's do it again soon.

PROLOGUE

Four years ago...

'HEY, MR LANDRY, what is it about British bad girls that makes them so hot, do you reckon...?'

Cade Landry stood in the Las Vegas event space, with the lights of the city's famous Strip glittering thirty-five storeys below them through the panoramic windows, nursing a glass of vintage bubbles which cost more than his first car, and scowled at the bad girl in question on the other side of the exclusive venue. She was dancing on a table, her slender figure moving in sensuous rhythm in a scrap of jewelled red satin which barely covered her butt.

'I don't know, Chad,' he shouted above the music from a world-famous DJ he'd paid to finish the evening with some fun after the formal event. Fun which was descending into a free-for-all thanks to the wild child and her posse. 'But whoever she is, she's leaving,' he added.

Exactly how old was she? Because she looked like an out-of-control kid who'd had one too many tequila slammers—and wasn't even legal to drink. He'd told security to get rid of them when they'd arrived ten minutes ago, but the guard looked as dazzled by her antics as the other guys around her.

'Don't you know who she is, Mr Landry?' Chad piped up again, his voice filling with awe. 'That's Charlotte Courtney.'

Damn.

He'd heard of Charlotte Courtney. Part-time model, full-time wild child, who'd hit the headlines hard a year ago when she'd chopped all her hair off and flounced out of a lucrative contract.

He dumped his glass on a passing tray and headed through the crowd, letting his temper build.

Yeah, Cade knew all about kids like Charlotte Courtney.

A poor little rich girl—who had never had to toe the line.

As a poor-boy-made-good from Louisiana, whose mom had kicked him into the system, age five, because feeding him had been too much trouble in between feeding her habit, he was the perfect person to teach her a lesson about how to behave herself. And not cause a ruckus in his place at his expense.

Which made the surge of protectiveness more than a little aggravating when a hand reached out from the crowd to slap her butt.

The girl swung round, her face a picture of outraged contempt, and kicked out at Mr Handsy. Cade could hear her giving the guy hell—in a British accent which was sharp enough to slice through flesh. The surge of protectiveness was joined by fury and an equally aggravating spurt of admiration for her.

He blocked another guy from getting too close as he reached the table, which had started to wobble.

'Take your hands off me, you creep,' Charlotte shouted at the man.

'How about I get you out of here, kid,' he bellowed to her above the music.

'Who are you?' she demanded. The flash of outrage in her eyes, though—which were a stunning, sparkling and surprisingly lucid emerald—had his admiration disappearing fast.

Who the hell did she think she was? Gate-crashing his event with a crew of hangers-on and behaving as if she owned the place?

'Cade Landry,' he shouted back. 'This is my place and my party. And as I didn't give you an invitation, I figure it's time you left.'

She scowled—obviously not liking his tone. So it caught him off guard when she shouted, 'Okay, thanks, Sir Galahad,' and took a flying leap off the table—and into his arms.

He staggered back, as no more than a hundred pounds of lithe female landed on top of him. He braced himself just in time to catch her, and stop them both from ending up on their butts. She looped her hands around his neck and wrapped her legs around his waist with impressive agility.

He inhaled a lungful of her scent—wild summer flowers and clean female sweat—for his pains. Her beautiful face—all high cheekbones and wide green eyes—broke into a grin.

'Well, don't just stand here, Galahad,' she demanded. 'Move. Before we end up as tomorrow's internet sensation.'

He didn't take orders from anyone any more, and especially not spoilt little rich girls. But Cade decided she had a point about the crowd as the cell phone lights blinked on around them.

Once he'd whisked her out of here, away from prying

camera phones, he could give her a piece of his mind. He set off through the crowd, forced to do the chivalrous thing, when he wasn't a chivalrous guy, his anger building with each stride.

Eventually, they made it into the elevator lobby, the music pounding behind them. Another security guard stood by the door.

'Mr Landry, sir?' he said, taking in the sight of the girl in Cade's arms just as her fingernails brushed across his nape—sending a jolt of something he didn't like one bit rippling through his system.

'Get the rest of them out of here, too,' he snarled. 'And tell your colleague he's been canned,' he added.

The man nodded and rushed back into the venue as Cade dropped his cargo onto her feet.

'Don't you think you're being a bit of a spoil-sport, Sir Galahad?' she said breathlessly, the playful glint in her translucent green eyes—the emerald hue reminding him of the Hand Grenade cocktails he'd once served by the dozen on Bourbon Street during Mardi Gras—telling him she didn't have one single clue how close she was to getting a damn spanking.

He'd worked eighteen-hour days, seven days a week, for over a decade to stop people judging him for a past he couldn't change, and she'd nearly trashed it all in a single night with her antics.

He stabbed the elevator call button. 'Ya think?' he growled.

'Yes, I do think,' she remarked in that crisp accent, which had a smoky purr which only added to his irritation. 'You seem quite uptight.'

She brushed the short cap of honey-brown curls back

from her face, and he noticed the smudge of glittery cosmetics that made her huge doe eyes look even bigger.

His gaze drifted down her figure. Her legs looked about a mile long thanks to the place mat–sized sparkly red dress and ankle-breaking heels. With the height boost from her footwear, her face was almost level with his, which, given that he was six-three, was a rarity. But despite her height, her body reminded him of a gazelle, slender and toned but also fragile. That she didn't have a bra on was something his body noted. And then discarded. His gaze snapped back to her face.

'Fair warning, kid,' he snarled. 'Next time you decide to shake your booty on a table, don't do it in my place.'

The flushed excitement on her face disappeared as her lips flattened, and her breasts rose and fell in a huff of outrage. Her stunning eyes narrowed, as if the Hand Grenade was about to detonate....

So little Miss Court Trouble wasn't used to being told no. *Tough.*

Cade Landry had no problem calling out reckless behaviour.

Surface beauty was just that, shallow and unearned. What mattered was a person's core. And from the things he'd seen so far, Charlotte Courtney was just like every other entitled rich kid who thought they were a grown-up but had no idea how to act like one.

Charley glared at the man sucking all the available oxygen out of the lobby area with his tall, dark, impossibly annoying handsomeness.

How typical... Charley Courtney's hunk in shining ar-

*mour turns out to have a judgemental streak as broad as
his mile-wide shoulders.*

'I see, and how do you plan to stop me, *exactly*?' she demanded, calling him on his self-righteousness.

She knew about Southern men and their manners.
She'd met a few after she'd been headhunted by a modelling agency at age sixteen—and ended up in the US working the catwalk while being hit on by a load of much older
guys. Of course, Cade Landry hadn't actually hit on her.
If anything, he had seemed surprisingly undazzled... But
give him time.

'How about we kick off with having you arrested for
underage drinking,' he replied, folding muscular forearms
over his chest and making the seams of his tuxedo bulge...
distractingly.

'How do you know I'm underage?' she demanded, determined to hold her own.

His gaze swept to her bottom with enough indifference
to make all her nerve endings stand on edge. 'Don't make
me laugh, kid.'

The way he said 'kid' in his Southern-fried accent
couldn't have sounded more condescending if he'd tried.
The judgemental approach was new, she'd give him that,
and somewhat unexpected. Men rarely tried to correct her
behaviour these days... But even so...

'I'm not a kid,' she sputtered. 'I'm eighteen.' In fact,
she'd turned eighteen that morning.

She'd only come out tonight with the guys from the
photoshoot in Caesars Palace to escape the direct hit of
her father's latest passive-aggressive text—one line in-
forming her he would have no time to see her when she
returned to London after her latest assignment. He hadn't

"Um… When exactly did I agree to move in with you?" she managed, annoyed by the he-who-shall-be-obeyed tone she was becoming far too familiar with.

"When you spent a good ten minutes throwing up this morning," he replied, flatly.

Her cheeks burned. Trust him to bring that up. "How is that relevant?"

Before she could follow up with all the reasons why it *so* wasn't, he had crossed the room and placed his palm on her cheek.

"Calm down, Charlotte," he said softly, the concerned tone as disturbing as the sudden urge to lean into his hand. "I don't want you on your own if you're sick again. That's all."

She pulled away from his touch. But she couldn't deny the wave of emotion threatening to sweep away her perfectly valid objections to his high-handed behavior. "This isn't even a real relationship," she added. "I'm just here as your stunt date for the summer."

He tucked his hand into his pocket, but his gaze remained fixed on her. "I think we've gone beyond that now, don't you?"

Billion-Dollar Bet

Three rival billionaires... Two huge problems...
One bet to solve them both!

Zane deMarco, Adam Courtney and Cade Landry
have two problems:

1. In their individual and ruthless pursuit of a failing
company, they're pushing the share price sky-high.

2. The billionaire playboys are being scandalously
called out online for their dating habits.

There's only one way to solve both... Whoever can
stay a one-woman man for the entire summer will
not only rid themselves of the rumors but add a new
company to their business portfolio.

They have a lot to lose, but a lot to gain. And what's
betting all of them also find passion worth risking it
all for?

Read Zane's story in
Billion-Dollar Dating Game by Natalie Anderson

Don't miss Adam's story
Boss with Benefits by Lucy King

And enjoy Cade's story
After-Party Consequences by Heidi Rice

All available now!

mentioned her birthday. But then, it wouldn't be the first time he'd forgotten.

Maybe her celebration had got a little out of hand, but no one else had tried to stop her. How typical that this man had appeared from the crowd like an avenging angel only to turn out to be a pompous ass...

Why Mr High and Mighty and his bulging biceps were having an unfortunate effect on her libido, though, she had no idea.

She hated to have her behaviour examined and found wanting by people who knew not one single thing about her life. Plus she didn't even *like* sex, because she had discovered—when she'd lost her virginity to a photographer after her first catwalk show in New York—it was totally overrated.

'That's still a kid from where I'm standing...' he said, but then she saw the flicker of something behind the cool expression.

'You think I'm a child? *Really?*' she challenged him, desperate to believe she'd seen something more than disdain.

His gaze darkened—and the frown on his brow became a crater.

He really was stupidly handsome. Tall and muscular with a shock of unruly black hair, his deep tan suggesting he either spent a lot of time sunbathing or he lived outdoors. She doubted he was an idle man, though, because his physique—and the way he had caught her and carried her out without breaking a sweat—appeared to have been forged in fire, rather than an expensive gym. The small scar which bisected his eyebrow and another visible through the stubble on his jaw made it obvious he hadn't led a charmed life. But then, neither had she. The only difference was her scars weren't visible.

Just when she thought she'd finally got the upper hand, the sexual tension snapping between them impossible for even Mr High and Mighty to deny, he huffed out a rough laugh. And the frown disappeared.

His firm lips kicked up in a wry smile so sensual it had her heartbeat sinking into her abdomen.

'Don't you think you've played with enough fire tonight, Charlotte?' he said as he unfolded his arms and leaned past her to press the button on the lift panel.

He loomed over her, forcing her to look up. A novel experience, because at five-foot-eleven in her heels, she was rarely at this much of a height disadvantage.

How did he know her name?

But then, she knew how, and struggled not to wince. Didn't everyone, after her meltdown at Paris Fashion Week a year ago?

'My name's Charley. No one calls me Charlotte,' she declared, determined not to be overwhelmed by his woodsy cologne, or the mouth-watering close-up of his Adam's apple, displayed against the open collar of his shirt alongside the flickering flames of an elaborate tattoo.

What would he do if she kissed him there, where the pulse in his throat throbbed in unison with the one in her panties?

His cool blue eyes turned to a searing sapphire, which made the pulsing awareness tense and melt at the same time. Surely he had to feel it too.

'I built this place, Charlotte,' he murmured. 'And I hosted the party you just tried to turn into a dumbass free-for-all...' He paused, clearly enjoying judging her—the hot, self-righteous jerk. 'With your childish behaviour.'

'*Childish…?*' she hissed, knowing she'd never been a child. Not really.

She yanked back her outrage when she spotted the sparkle of amusement in his eyes. Was he deliberately trying to wind her up? Because it was totally working.

His cheeks tensed. He was waging a battle not to laugh, something he was struggling to hide.

Adrenaline surged up her torso. Why she found the spark of connection so thrilling, she had no idea. It had been a long time since she'd been attracted to any guy. Or had the desire to flirt with one. But something about Cade Landry—and his determination to see her as a girl instead of a woman—called to her inner demons.

She wanted to taste those lips so badly. Wanted to make him admit he saw her and she mattered. What would it be like to have those sensual lips taking hers in a ruthless kiss? Exciting? Exhilarating? Validating?

The throbbing in her sex matched the rush of blood in her ears. She breathed in a lungful of his delicious scent—man and musk and pine woods. A sob of surrender slipped from her lips, inviting him in.

She lifted her arm and curled her fingers around his nape. 'Kiss me, Landry,' she whispered, the feeling of empowerment making her feel euphoric. 'You know you want to.'

But instead of covering her lips with his, he took her hand from around his neck and stepped back, the contempt in his eyes unmistakeable.

'Kiss you?' he murmured. The euphoria in her belly became sharp and jagged—the distaste in his tone something she'd heard before from her father. 'Why the hell would I want to kiss an off-the-rails kid with an attitude problem?'

The lift doors swished open behind her, the sound masked by the brutal thunder of her heartbeat.

'Now get out of my place, before I call the cops,' he finished, the disgust in his eyes searing her soul.

She stared, speechless with humiliation, as he turned and walked back into the event without a backward glance.

She rushed into the lift, suddenly desperate to get away from him—and the rejection echoing in her ears. She stabbed at the button, the hot, angry tears burning her eyeballs. She bit into her lip to stop them falling as the lift doors closed at last.

She hadn't cried since the day her mother had died, when she was eight years old. She certainly didn't intend to let a few harsh words from a staid, boring, self-righteous jerk with a superiority complex make her cry now.

But as the luminous glitter of the neon cityscape was revealed in the glass wall on the far side of the lift, Cade Landry's sharp words echoed over and over again in her head. Her stomach dropped like a stone, the stunning view of Las Vegas only making her feel smaller and more foolish and insignificant.

She wanted to hate Cade Landry for being as cruel and dismissive as her father. Why should she care if he didn't see her? Didn't want her? When other men did?

But as the scenic elevator tracked down the side of the building, and the miserable sinking sensation in her stomach bottomed out at her toes, instead of feeling righteous and fierce and independent, all she really felt was how she'd felt throughout her childhood. Vulnerable…and unlovable…and invisible…and hideously alone.

CHAPTER ONE

July 4, the present

CADE LANDRY WRAPPED a towel around his waist, ready to head into the sauna behind his squash buddies, Zane de-Marco and Adam Courtney. They met every couple of weeks to thrash out their frustrations on the court. But that wasn't the only reason he was here today.

Courtney had suggested a meet-up to discuss...*something*?

Being a cagey Brit, the guy hadn't specified what, but Cade could make an educated guess. He had his suspicions both deMarco and Courtney were involved in the recent spike in the share price of Helberg Holdings. Courtney probably wanted them both to give him a free run... But no way in hell was that happening.

Helberg was a heritage brand—old-school, traditional, with a legacy which went way back. The company also had a real estate portfolio to die for, which Cade knew Landry Construction could bring back to its former glory.

Now Reed Helberg was dead, the company and all its assets were up for grabs. Owning that name, that history, that legacy would prove Landry Construction had class, something money alone couldn't buy, and would finally allow

Cade to reclaim a miserable memory from his childhood, which Helberg had incidentally been a part of.

No way was anyone taking Helberg away from him. Not even his squash buddies…

But as Cade went to shut his locker, his phone buzzed. A text from Dan Carmichael, the CEO of the PR consultancy he had hired to work on brand management for the planned Helberg buyout, appeared on screen.

He lifted the phone back out of his gym bag. And scowled.

Cade, we have a problem. Have you seen the puff piece in Blush about you and deMarco and Courtney? It's getting a lot of traction on social media. I'm not sure being called out as one of the #OneDateWonder billionaires is what we want for the brand atm.

OneDateWonder? What the…?

He clicked on the link Dan had added, because he had never heard of a magazine called *Blush*. He scoured the headline, then the piece itself—which was illustrated with a host of snapped shots of him and Adam and Zane at a string of events in the last couple of months with a lot of different dates. And cursed. Loudly.

His chest tightened and his blood pressure spiked, his fury matched by the frustrating sense of impotence, as he scanned the comments on social media which Dan had also flagged.

Apparently, he, deMarco, and Courtney were at the centre of a gathering viral storm, featuring a bunch of insulting hashtags—*#OneDateWonders, #billionaireblueeyed-*

boysclub, #mancandysummer and *#catchthemifyoucan*
among them.

The internet debate, focussed exclusively on their sex
lives, made all three of them look like jerks.

Could this derail what he wanted to achieve with Helberg?

Making Landry Construction respectable, aspirational,
and the leading brand in high-class luxury properties was
his life's work. But just when he was about to take the next
step, the *final* step, some dumb magazine article had decided to turn his private life into a dirty joke.

He slung his cell in his gym bag and slammed the locker
door.

He could take a joke as well as the next guy, but having
his private life ridiculed reminded him way too forcefully
of being mocked as the only kid in senior high who didn't
have a prom date—because he couldn't afford a corsage,
let alone tux hire. He wasn't that cast-off kid any more. He
could buy whatever he wanted now. But he'd be damned if
he'd let anyone laugh at him for clickbait.

He walked into the sauna and dropped onto the bench
opposite Courtney. The view of the Manhattan skyline
through the treated glass reminded him of how far he'd
come since being shunted around a string of small towns
in Louisiana—a the foster kid nobody had wanted to keep.

He cut off the pity party in his head as he picked up on
the conversation between Zane and Adam. Didn't take long
to figure out his hunch had been right about Courtney's motives for calling this meeting when the Brit added, 'I need
you both to back off...'

'Helberg? Not happening...' Cade said bluntly.

'No can do,' Zane added, making Adam Courtney frown.

'It's a once in a lifetime opportunity, y'all,' Cade drawled.

He didn't let on he had personal skin in this game. Revealing how important it was to him to buy the company would make him look weak. And while he liked these guys well enough, they weren't *that* close. Plus, he knew they both had a killer instinct—from the way they played squash.

'Then we have a problem,' said Courtney with a gravity Cade had come to expect from the guy. After all, he'd inherited his family's business at twenty-eight.

He certainly had a lot more gravity than his kid sister, Charlotte, Cade thought ruefully, recalling something he'd discovered a couple months back.

Adam Courtney was the older brother of the poor little rich girl he'd crossed swords with in Vegas four years back and had never been able to forget…completely.

The family connection had been a surprise. Cade would not have put the measured, well-spoken, close-lipped guy sweating manfully opposite him together with the wild child who'd been shaking her booty on a table. Cade had never spoken about that long-ago encounter with Courtney because he'd been trying to forget the girl's luminous green eyes, her fragile beauty, and her inappropriate come-on ever since.

So why the hell are you thinking about her now?

'Actually, we have problems. Plural,' Cade said. He needed to focus on that article and not his close encounter with Courtney's sister—which was ancient history.

'What the hell are you talking about?' Adam replied, with just enough frustration to rile Cade.

'Clearly you don't read *Blush*,' Cade growled.

'The women's magazine?' Adam looked nonplussed,

clearly not as clueless as Cade about trashy celeb culture. 'You read that?'

'No, I don't read it,' Cade snarled…because…*really*? 'But my PR consultant does. He just texted me. Did y'all know we are the star players in their latest dumb article? "The Billionaire Bachelors Least Likely to Marry." Apparently, we three have been tagged the One Date Wonders… The guys with the longest odds, and they've already started a tally on how many dates we'll have racked up by Labor Day.'

'You're kidding?' Zane said, looking more amused than outraged. 'Who I date is no one's business but mine. And I'm not going to stop—I've no plans to settle down. Ever.'

'Neither do I,' Adam added, not sounding remotely amused.

Me either, Cade thought but didn't add.

'They're turning our sex lives into a joke—and getting a lot of traction,' Cade continued. 'And that's not the kind of media attention I want for my business. Do you?' he finished.

He hadn't worked his butt off his whole life to be taken seriously only to garner this kind of attention.

'Exactly how much traction are we talking about?' Zane asked, the smug grin gone.

'The hashtag One Date Wonders is the top trending topic in the US on most of the main apps today. That much,' Cade answered. 'And just about every American female online seems to have an opinion now about our sex lives… We're basically the red meat at the centre of a social media feeding frenzy.'

Adam winced. Zane looked thoughtful for once.

'My PR team are freaking out about it,' Cade continued.

'Personally, I don't give a damn what a bunch of clickbait junkies and their enablers think of my dating habits…' Except he did, kind of, or the article wouldn't have made him so mad. 'But no way in hell am I letting anyone make me look like a jerk who can't keep his junk in his pants.'

'We need to find a way to shut it down,' Courtney said.

Silence fell. But as the temperature in the sauna rose, so did the hackles on the back of Cade's neck…

Maybe deMarco and Courtney weren't *as* pissed about the hit to their reputations, but then, they'd never had to fight for respect the way Cade had. Courtney came by it naturally, being from old money in the UK, and deMarco was enough of a bad boy not to give a damn what anyone thought about him.

But Cade did give a damn. And somehow, the more he thought about it, the more furious and frustrated he became.

'What if we take ourselves off the market?' Zane offered, with the reckless twinkle in his eyes Cade recognised from when he was about to make a killer shot on the squash court.

'Forget it,' Cade said. Was deMarco nuts? 'No way am I *actually* getting hitched to shut this down.'

'Absolutely not… It's out of the question,' Adam concurred.

At least two of them hadn't gone to the dark side.

'Did I say anything about getting hitched?' Zane said, as if they were both fools. 'This is a countdown, right? So how about we stop the clock before it even starts. All we have to do is date one woman—and one woman only— from now until Labor Day. Simple.'

'You're kidding. You actually want to pander to this garbage?' Cade said, a little astonished. Having his sex life ridiculed on social media was bad, but having to curtail it to suit some glossy rag's clickbait agenda was worse.

'Not particularly, but I'm betting you two are going to break long before I do,' Zane said, with that feral glint still in his eyes.

'I'll take that bet, because the last time I looked, you're a bigger serial dater than the both of us,' Cade replied wryly.

'You don't even know what the stake is,' Adam pointed out. As if they were actually going to bet on their sex lives…

'My Helberg shares,' Zane shot back, surprising the hell out of Cade, but also making his heartbeat slow—the way it did whenever he was about to close on a sweet property deal.

'Hold on a minute. You'd bet on Helberg?' Cade asked, sure he could not have heard that right. 'Are you serious?'

deMarco's feral grin answered the question before he did. 'Sure. Why not? It's Independence Day today,' Zane continued. 'What if we meet back here on Labor Day. Winner takes all accumulated shares and has an unimpeded run at Helberg.'

Cade frowned. *Damn*. Despite how uncomfortable it made him feel letting the press dictate his sex life for the summer, the bet was mighty tempting. It provided a way for the three of them to square off over Helberg without driving the share price up any higher—while also nipping all the unwanted social media attention in the bud and minimising the hit to their reputations.

And best of all, Cade could totally win this bet.

Given deMarco's track record with dates, he was at least as much of a hound dog as Cade. Courtney was a dark horse who also had a lot more class than the two of them, but Cade would still take his chances.

Especially when Courtney hissed, 'Have you completely lost your mind?'

And it occurred to Cade that if Courtney was anywhere near as reckless as his kid sister, keeping it in his pants wasn't going to be any easier for him than his buddy Zane.

The arrogant thought had the picture of those stunning emerald eyes swirling through Cade's memory again... But now, instead of the fragile strung-out kid, he couldn't help wondering...

What *would* she be like now? Because he'd heard whispers she had cleaned up her act and stopped modelling a while back.

He cut off his curiosity, though, along with the strange surge of adrenaline.

Get a clue, Landry.

Charlotte Courtney might be four years older, but she was probably just as much of a handful. There was a reason why he preferred women who were sophisticated, mature and predictable. Something he suspected the former British bad girl would never be...

Zane hitched his shoulder in a confident shrug. 'This *Blush* business is an annoyance, right? But I'm more interested in sorting out which of us gets Helberg. This is a good way to take you guys on and beat you once and for all. Two birds, one stone.'

'It's nuts,' Cade had to admit. 'But it also makes sense.'

Could he do it, though? More than two months, dating only one woman?

The prospect didn't fill him with joy. He liked sex. It was

one of the few recreational activities he allowed himself. And he enjoyed the thrill of the chase even more…

'It's ridiculous.' Courtney did not sound happy.

Okay, so now Courtney sounded like he was protesting way too much.

Cade rarely dated the same woman twice—because it tended to give them ideas of the eligible bachelor variety—but he could make an exception for a few months. There had to be a woman who could hold his interest for more than a couple of dates. And not every woman was looking for a commitment. All he had to do was find the right one.

'You got a better idea?' Zane fired back. 'Because the likelihood of us stepping out of each other's way just because you asked nicely is…*what*?'

Cade couldn't help it, he laughed. 'Afraid you'll lose, Courtney?'

He found himself relishing the challenge of going up against these two, already calculating the logistics of how to win the bet.

He was headed to the Bay Area this afternoon, to check out some of the properties in the Helberg portfolio on the West Coast which were ripe for redevelopment—in the hope of closing this deal soon. Why not scope out suitable dating options over the weekend at the same time? Seeing as he was going to be based mostly on the West Coast for the summer, it made sense to hook up with someone on that side of the country.

Plus, he'd had an invite tonight to the lavish Fourth of July bash tech billionaire and fellow Louisiana native Luke Broussard and his wife, Cassandra, hosted every year on the estate Landry Construction had built for them and their ever-expanding family in Marin County. Cade hadn't intended to go. With three children at the last count, the Broussards tended to invite a lot of families to their events and, as a rule, Cade didn't do families. But the evening bash was an adults-only affair—which had a reputation for being exclusive and private as well as fun and informal. The perfect place to start looking for a woman who was engaging enough to hold his attention until Labor Day in early September, but who was also as commitment-phobic as he was—without getting caught on camera before he had made a choice.

Thoughts of Charlotte Courtney popped up again, reminding him of a rumour he'd heard that she was a friend of Broussard's wife, Cassie, another aristocratic Brit and a successful entrepreneur. Hadn't Luke told him Cassie had bought a dress from her because the former wild child had started some kind of fashion brand?

He frowned. Why the heck had he even remembered that?

Okay, maybe he *was* a tiny bit more than just curious about how that kid had turned out, and whether or not she had *really* managed to turn her life around, but that was it. The last thing he needed for his summer date was some-one volatile or reckless or confrontational—even if she was pretending to be a businesswoman now, instead of just a bratty kid.

'Not at all,' her brother, Adam, replied, with a tiny hint of superiority which probably came with all that stellar breeding, something his sister sure as hell hadn't inher-ited. 'Quite the opposite,' he added. 'So, just to clarify: we date one woman each, between now and Labor Day. Any-one caught dating more than one woman in that time re-linquishes their claim on Helberg?'

'Right. I'm in,' deMarco concurred.

'You're on,' Cade replied, shoving the unhelpful thoughts of Adam's kid sister out of his head. He doubted she remembered him with much positivity either, given the expression on her face—angry and devastated at the same time—when he'd given it to her straight about her behaviour four years ago. So the smart move would be to give her a wide berth if she did happen to turn up at Luke's bash. And Cade prided himself on always making the smart move.

Adam stared at them both. Then a smile curved his lips. 'May the best man win,' he declared.

Cade nodded and smiled back—because he intended to do whatever it took to ensure the best man would be him.

CHAPTER TWO

That night

CHARLEY TOOK AN unsteady breath as she stepped out of the taxi onto the torchlit lawn of the staggering stone-and-glass mansion on the Tiburon Peninsula.

Built on an extensive piece of untouched land in Marin County, the Broussards' home had spectacular views. The lack of any nearby developments afforded the guests, as they walked to the dramatic arched entrance, a panoramic vista which included Angel Island, the Golden Gate and Bay Bridges, and San Francisco's towering skyline across the water.

Charley was no stranger to luxury living, or the parties of the rich and famous. After all, she'd once been one of their number, in her own backhanded fashion. But she'd learned the hard way to hate that life—the wild parties, the endless hotel rooms, the long workdays and even longer play nights which had eventually become a blur of over-indulgence, anxiety, and exhaustion, sucking up all of her adolescence.

She lived frugally now, in a flat in London's up-and-coming East End bought from her earnings as a model—her new life funded by the trickle of revenue from the growing cache of exclusive clients she had managed to impress with her innovative and eclectic dress designs.

Her passion for fashion was one of the few upsides of her short-lived career as a teenage catwalk model, which had mostly just exposed the ugly grit behind the glamour of the industry. But after three years at fashion college in London, learning her craft as a bespoke designer, and an end-of-year show which had piqued the interest of Cassandra Broussard—enough for the tech billionaire's influential wife to become her first buyer—she was now set to finally make a success of her life...on her own terms.

So when Cassandra's email had dropped into her in-box, inviting her, oh-so-casually, to one of the most sought-after and exclusive social events of the summer on America's West Coast, she'd maxed out her credit card to buy an economy class ticket to San Francisco International—and spent every spare evening in the meantime sewing by hand the cocktail dress she was currently wearing—without a single hesitation.

All she needed to do now was model the design at the Broussards' party, without making it too obvious she was touting for business...

Cassandra had handed her a golden opportunity to showcase her signature design style with the exclusive Silicon Valley crowd who were Charley's dream clientele. Now, if she could just get a handle on the butterflies in her stomach, which had turned into dive-bombers on the flight across the Atlantic...

She brushed shaky palms down the bronze silk which stopped mid-thigh and tucked the matching purse under her arm, thinking momentarily about all the hours she had spent painstakingly sewing on the beading.

*Look confident. And no one will know you're terrified
of doing this sober!*

The ankle boots she'd chosen to go with the dress—because, for a garden party, heels were definitely out—clicked
on the stone path in time with her rampaging heartbeat.
She took a deep breath and offered the uniformed security
guard a bright smile along with the QR code on her phone.

The man nodded after checking her ID, then handed her
over to a young woman in a tailored suit—who beamed
at her.

'Miss Courtney, I'm Alex Burley, Mrs Broussard's assistant. Luke and Cassie are delighted you could join them
tonight. Would you like me to give you a tour of the estate,
or do you want to go straight through to the party? There's
a lounge area by the pool, cocktails on the terrace, or the
band, who have started a dance set in the garden.'

'Brilliant, Alex, thanks,' Charley said with a confidence
she didn't feel, but had learned how to fake years ago.

She needed to locate Cassie and say thanks to her personally for the invite, and the opportunity. But the sound
of the music coming from below the house—a joyous if
unfamiliar mix of R&B and rock 'n' roll accompanied by
some insane fiddles—was undeniably infectious.

'Actually, I'd love to check out the band,' she said, because she needed to loosen up before she started networking.

'Good choice.' Alex beamed some more, then led her
around the house before excusing herself.

Charley walked down stone steps into the garden, enchanted by the informal surroundings—which had the vibe
of a music festival rather than a posh society party.

Fairy lights adorned the arbour of trees and twinkled in

the glimmer of twilight, framing the view across San Francisco Bay and making it magical as well as breathtaking. The fast-paced fiddles had been joined by an accordion on the stage, and the dulcet tones of a singer—whose throaty French patois seemed to sink into Charley's soul—had her heels tapping of their own accord.

But what enchanted Charley more was how unself-conscious everyone seemed. As if they were enjoying the chance to let off steam, rather than trying to be seen.

The throng of guests chatted and laughed, drinking more beer than champagne, while a huge hog roast was being served on the level above the stage. The dance floor had been laid out under the stars, and was packed with people young and old, some famous, most not, wearing everything from jeans and T-shirts to boho dresses and designer couture as they twirled and boogied in a couples' dance.

In the centre of the mêlée were Luke and Cassandra Broussard.

Charley's pulse kicked against her throat, and she felt weightless for a moment—which had to be her excitement at the stellar business opportunity tonight's event presented, and not the romantic sight of the Broussards dancing together in joyous unison, as if they were completely alone.

She didn't believe in love. Her own parents' marriage—from the little she could remember of it—had been a disaster. And her brother, Adam, had never managed to hold down a serious relationship as far as she knew.

But even so, Charley found herself spellbound.

Cassandra Broussard was a brilliant businesswoman who was warm and kind, and also impossibly serene and sophisticated. But tonight, wearing a summer dress which floated around her body as her husband launched her into a twirl, she looked incandescent. When she threw back her head and laughed at something her husband had whispered in her ear, Charley had the weirdest urge to believe what the Broussards shared was real and would last, when Charley had never had such a cheesy thought in her entire life.

Not even as a little girl.

Especially as a little girl. The vague memory of her mother's broken sobbing and her father's brutal criticisms soured the happy glow.

'Hello, Charlotte. Why aren't you on the dance floor?'

The low, husky voice at her earlobe had Charley swinging round to find a fierce blue gaze she recognised locked on her.

'Or better yet, on one of the tables,' he added, his Southern drawl edged with amusement.

Sensation streaked through her, burning away the last of the romantic glow.

'Cade Landry, what an unpleasant surprise,' she murmured, then wanted to kick herself when the rich sapphire of his irises twinkled like the damn fairy lights.

Fabulous! The man had caught her totally off guard, or she never would have admitted she remembered him or that brutal humiliation from four years ago.

She swallowed, trying to stifle the unwelcome sensations already making the hair on her neck tingle with awareness.

She'd been eighteen and seriously messed up back then, or she never would have thrown herself at him and exposed herself to his ridicule. She was twenty-two now and had left that miserable phase of her life behind—weirdly enough as a direct result of his brutal rejection, which had finally made her confront how far out of control her life had become and how vulnerable she had made herself to men like him. But she would rather die than admit to him that his cruel slap down had helped turn her life around. Because she doubted he'd care. Plus, she had stopped looking for approval in all the wrong places… Especially from overbearing billionaires like Cade Landry, who—from the amused, indulgent expression on his handsome face—still had an ego the size of Las Vegas and the rough-hewn, rugged muscles to match…

Rough-hewn…rugged…? What the heck?

What was she doing noticing the defined contours of his chest through the tight white T-shirt, and his long legs and lean waist displayed to perfection in worn jeans?

She didn't do needy and desperate any more. And she didn't get turned on by anyone—however fit they might be—because in her limited experience, sex was about as much fun as a root canal.

So stop checking out his pecs, then.

'How about you dance with me and we test that theory?' he said, with an audacity she should have expected from a player like him.

She'd read all about Landry and her brother, Adam, and Adam's mate Zane deMarco, and their giddy dating shenanigans in an article on the plane…which would have been funny if it hadn't been illustrated with so many candid photos of the man in front of her with a host of different women on his arm. Beautiful, smart, stunning, sophisticated women…

Making her far too aware of how swiftly he'd slapped down her clumsy attempts to seduce him, once upon a time. Okay, she'd been off the rails and screwed-up, but he hadn't needed to be so cruel.

'What theory would that be?' she asked, annoyed by the adrenaline spike at the sparkle in his eyes.

'The theory that you and I can't be friends now, Charlotte,' he said.

'*Friends?* Really? You think we can be friends? Have you forgotten how you kicked me out of your place four years ago? Because—FYI—I haven't.' Good grief, did he really think she wanted to give him an opportunity to slap her down all over again? She might be a lot more resilient now, a lot more aware of her own worth, but she wasn't a masochist, or an idiot.

But then his gruff chuckle at her snarky response made her heartbeat accelerate. Disconcerting her.

'Sure, why not? Aren't you a woman now, Charlotte, instead of a kid?' he said, the provocative question entirely deliberate. Was he coming on to her?

She should be insulted, but she wasn't...*quite*. Which was even more disconcerting... But then, Cade Landry was an exceptionally hot guy—and unfortunately, he knew it.

'Actually, I was a woman back then,' she said, because she owed it to that wayward girl to defend her. 'You just didn't have the guts to handle me.'

His eyebrows launched up his forehead. And she congratulated herself on the direct hit. But then his lips curved, and his hot gaze roamed over her. Not with disdain this time, but with approval, which was a great deal more disturbing.

Her sex clenched and released, just as it had four years ago, a response she'd never felt for any other man.

Oh... Hell. Seriously?

'Sounds to me like you've held a grudge for four years because I wouldn't kiss you,' he said.

'Sounds to me like your ego is still the size of Pluto,' she shot straight back, refusing to confirm or deny. Maybe she had been devastated at the time—disproportionate to his actual crimes—because she'd been so vulnerable then, behind the bad girl pose. But he'd still been an overbearing humourless arse, so there was that.

'Touché, Charlotte,' he said, the teasing tone tempting now, rather than judgey. 'How about I say sorry for being so blunt last time we met…and we start over.'

It wasn't much of an apology, but somehow, it helped to ease her anxiety at seeing him again, and being reminded of that awful encounter in Vegas.

He held out his hand. 'Dance with me…' he asked again, the glow in those searing sapphire eyes hot enough to thaw the polar ice cap.

The urge to accept his invitation—simply to rewrite that chapter in her misspent youth, she told herself staunchly—had the anxiety downgrading even more…

But then the band dived into another fast-paced song. The couples on the floor whirled around, their intricate steps a dance Charley had never seen before—and knew she couldn't pull off without making a fool of herself.

She'd once loved dancing, on tables especially, but sobriety had made her less of an extrovert. And she didn't want to end up on her backside wearing her signature dress. Especially not in front of Mr Ego-the-Size-of-Pluto.

'Of course, I would totally take you up on your generous offer,' she lied without a qualm. 'But I'm not sure I should help you get one up on my brother so soon in the One Date Wonder stakes.'

He winced. 'Is there anyone who has not read that damn article?'

She chuckled, surprised to have found a chink in his armour without even trying. 'You aren't flattered?'

She'd always assumed guys like him loved to flaunt their playboy image.

Her father had cheated on her mother with impunity and made no attempt to hide it. After her mother's death, his sordid sex life had even threatened to bring down the family business. But it had taken years for him to be held to account. Cade Landry, on the other hand, looked genuinely uncomfortable.

'Flattered? At having my dating history ridiculed for clickbait?' he scoffed. 'No. Would you be?'

'Of course not,' she replied. 'But the standards are different for women. Especially...' She raised her fingers to do air quotes. 'An "off the rails kid with an attitude problem".' She placed her hand on her hip. 'And, if I recall correctly, you judged me accordingly when you met me.'

'Charlotte, you were drunk, underage, and shaking your booty on a table at two a.m. when I met you. So you weren't doing a whole heck of a lot to challenge that assumption.'

'I wasn't drunk,' she said in her defence.

Because I remember every single detail of that encounter with far too much clarity.

'But getting back to you...' she continued, because Cade Landry did not need to know how often she'd thought about him. Or that his brutal dismissal of her charms back then had been the wake-up call she'd needed to stop making a spectacle of herself and confirming everyone's low expectations. The man's ego was enormous enough. 'You're not doing a whole heck of a lot to challenge that article by asking me to dance when you were photographed with Jenna Carmody two nights ago at the Met.'

She thought she had him bang to rights. But instead of looking chastened, his sensual smile returned—which only made him look more delicious. *The rat.*

'Have you been keeping tabs on me, Charlotte?' he asked, with the same arrogance she remembered. But why did his attitude towards her feel exhilarating now, rather than critical?

'I don't need to keep tabs on you…' she fired back. 'Your dating history is kind of hard to miss.'

'Fair point,' he murmured. Before she could congratulate herself, though, he added, 'Although Jenna and I aren't dating. She's in a long-term relationship, and she only came to the gala as my plus-one because her partner, Melanie, had the flu.'

'I'm pretty sure that still qualifies as a date,' Charley said, trying to maintain the argument, but oddly disarmed that he had bothered to explain the situation.

'Not in all the ways that count,' he said, his voice becoming a husky purr. His gaze took on that hot glow again, and his hand reappeared. 'This dance, on the other hand, has a lot more potential…'

The seductive tone was back with a vengeance. She couldn't deny the powerful urge to say yes any more. Forcing her to come clean.

'I'd love to accept…' She glanced at the dance floor, where the band had begun another high-tempo number. 'But I can't…'

'Why the heck not?'

'Because I've never danced like that. I don't even know what kind of music they're playing…even though I think it sounds fabulous.'

'It's Zydeco. Because Luke is a Cajun boy from the

Bayou Teche.' The devastating smile became a devastating grin. 'You've really never danced the Cajun two-step?'

'Nope,' she said. 'There aren't a lot of Cajuns in Shoreditch,' she added, which was where she lived in East London.

'Then you've missed out.' He beckoned her again with those long, strong fingers. 'I can teach you to Zydeco. All you have to do is follow my lead…like a good girl.'

Four years ago, the provocative comment would have inflamed her rebellious nature, but now all it did was inflame her senses—the wicked glint in his eyes tempting her to share the joke rather than become the butt of it.

She suddenly had a vision of following Cade Landry's lead in other ways.

The man *was* a bona fide player, but he was currently unattached, and into her. And she'd once wanted him desperately. She'd never envisioned wanting him again—not after that brutal rejection—but the liquid pull in her abdomen was impossible to ignore as he waited for her to take the bait…or chicken out. Maybe dancing with him now could be a reward for making the changes to become, if not a good girl, then at least much more together now than she had been that night in Vegas.

In the interest of full disclosure, she added, 'I'm terrible at following anyone's lead. And I've always found good girls remarkably dull.'

He laughed, the rich sound making the heat in her abdomen throb. Then he captured her fingers, his warm skin rough against hers as he tugged her towards him.

'That sounds like a challenge I can't resist,' he said as he lifted her hand and buzzed a kiss across her palm.

The jolt of heat arrowed down. The intense gaze was

something she recognised from long ago, but it wasn't cold this time. It was scorching her skin in the most delicious way possible.

'Okay. I'll dance with you.' She grinned, feeling daring for the first time in a long time. 'But be warned, you might lose a few of your toes.'

'I've always figured toes are like good girls...' he declared as he led her onto the moonlit dance floor. 'Overrated.'

'It's just an easy two-step, but with more of a booty sway...' Cade clasped Charlotte's left hand and placed his free hand on her waist to direct her movements. 'But let's not get too fancy right off.'

'Yes, let's definitely not do that!' she remarked, her face a picture of concentration as he showed her the forward and backward steps, and helped her to roll her hips in time with the music. 'I do not want to fall on my arse in this dress,' she added.

He laughed, the comment as infectious as the scent of her—sultry and fresh—on the night air. And the feel of her in his arms.

'And it's such a nice arse,' he offered, using the British word.

He'd been determined to avoid Charlotte Courtney if she showed up at Luke's party. He had important business tonight if he was going to secure a summer date to win the bet.

But the second he'd laid eyes on her, strolling into the garden wearing a wisp of a dress which hugged her slender curves, the rush of adrenaline had been followed by a heady shot of desire. And all the reasons why he shouldn't

approach her and shouldn't pander to his curiosity about
her had flown right out of his head and drifted away on
the warm sea breeze.

After their ten-minute conversation, he'd made the
welcome discovery the fragile, lawless girl had become a
stunning, strong and forthright woman—her brittle edges
replaced by a refreshing sass.

She moved with the same easy rhythm he remembered
from when she'd danced on that table, but she seemed more
circumspect now—which only charmed him more.

The band launched into an old Cajun classic, full of
rhythm and swing—the fiddles joined by bass guitar and
the whine of a harmonica. The dance floor was packed,
and the slower tempo allowed him to hold her closer. But as
the familiar musical lilts flowed through him, she tensed.

'Relax, Charlotte. Ain't nobody grading you, I swear.'

Her gaze, which had been locked on her feet, met his.
He found himself drowning in that bright green gaze, her
lips a feast he wanted to taste so badly his mouth watered.
Ironic, given that when she'd offered them to him four years
ago, he'd been appalled.

She grinned. 'Easy for you to say.' But she softened
enough to brush against him in a sensuous rhythm, which
could get awkward fast.

He lifted her arm and stepped back. 'Go for it,' he murmured, and she took the hint.

Her ripple of laughter as she spun round under his arm
was almost as intoxicating as the breathless excitement on
her face when she landed the turn and slapped her palm
against his chest to regain her balance.

He launched her into another twirl.

'Enough!' she chuckled as she fell back into his arms.

HEIDI RICE   41

Damn, but she was delicious, and a remarkably fast learner.

He imagined a host of other things he would love to teach her...

Whoa, boy. Don't go getting ahead of yourself.

He needed to find the perfect summer date, and Charlotte would always be an unknown quantity. Plus she was based in the UK, so however attracted he was right now, she wasn't likely to be the woman who could help him win Helberg. But who said he had to find his date tonight? Why not just enjoy himself—and satisfy his curiosity once and for all?

He clasped her waist, anchoring her hips, as the band dived into another tune. Their easy moves became more potent, more passionate, a dance of ecstasy and joy. The swift streak of heat and excitement felt familiar and yet entirely new as they moved to the beat—and she lost her inhibitions, becoming bolder and brighter and more dazzling.

When was the last time he'd danced the Zydeco? And taken the time to relax and enjoy himself with a woman who fascinated him? He picked up the pace, captivated when she followed his lead effortlessly, and added some booty shakes that had his senses reeling as fast at the fiddles.

The soft, silky dress and the firm, toned flesh beneath moved against his palm as they pressed closer, the dance floor filling, the heat rising.

Time faded as the night flew past in a haze of sensation.

By the time they'd danced for almost an hour, they were both breathing hard, covered in a light sweat in the muggy night. The press of the other bodies, the scent of burning pork and salt on the sea air was underlaid with the sultry perfume of flowers and female sweat.

She laughed up at him. 'This is so fun!' she said, her excitement clear and uninhibited. 'But I can't believe I haven't crippled you.'

'You're a natural,' he said, tugging her back towards him. Her palm flattened against his chest as the band's set moved into a slow dance. He settled his hand on her hip to hold her close. She didn't protest.

Her body pressed so intimately against his made the heat pound. Her eyes widened. Was she aware of the reaction he couldn't control? Her lips parted, reminding him of their meeting four years ago, except that this time, they were irresistible.

But as the last note died, and the band announced they were taking a break, she stepped away from him.

He knew they probably ought to cool off, him especially, but he heard himself ask, 'How about some hog roast?'

He waited patiently for her answer, while not feeling patient at all. Something had happened on the dance floor, something vivid and potent—and mutual. She'd captivated him, that much was obvious, but he needed time to think before he acted on this attraction. And considered all the angles. Even so, he knew he wasn't ready to let her go.

Her face glowed from their recent exertion, but her expression became wary.

'I should start networking,' she said with a candour he had not expected. 'To justify the exorbitant cost of my airfare.'

'Is this about your designer brand?'

'You know about that?' Her face flushed with pleasure, and he realised her business couldn't be the vanity project he'd assumed it was when Luke had mentioned it.

'Luke told me you made a dress for his wife, and she loved it.'

Her face glowed. 'Yes, I did. I'm so pleased he told you that. Cassandra Broussard has been wonderful. I'm sure she only invited me tonight because she knew how much it could boost my business...'

'How so?' he asked, genuinely intrigued.

He wished now he'd taken the time to check her out on the internet—something he'd avoided to convince himself he wasn't *that* interested in her.

'I'm modelling one of my own designs,' she said, giving him an impromptu twirl, and filling his senses with another lungful of her intoxicating scent. 'What do you think?'

'Stunning,' he said. Although he couldn't help thinking while the dress was pretty enough, the woman inside was the real stunner.

Her grin widened. 'You see, that's exactly the reaction I was hoping for. But I need to get myself in front of all the potential clients here—who would be mostly female—and wow them with this dress, so they want to commission me,' she added breathlessly. Then she chewed her lip. 'Although...' She glanced around as people filed past them, heading for the dining tables set up by the treeline or the terraces above. 'I really did not expect anything like this.'

'Like what?' he asked, enchanted by the flush on her cheeks and the fierce purpose in her eyes.

'Something fun and not at all formal. It feels a bit rude now to start touting for business, even incidentally...'

He captured her hand. 'How about we eat some burnt pig while you tell me who you want to target,' he said. 'I may not need a designer gown,' he added. 'But I know most of the women here. So I can introduce you around.'

'Is that a good idea?' she said, sounding doubtful. 'I

want to sell bespoke haute couture by Trouble Maker, not piss off all your former lovers.'

'Hey.' He choked out a gruff laugh. 'First off, we're not dating…' *Yet.* 'Second, I don't sleep with every woman I date. And last but not least, I'm not so prolific that I know every woman in the Bay Area in a biblical sense. You shouldn't believe everything you read.'

'Duly noted.' She looked suitably chastened, but then she smiled. 'You really don't mind introducing me around?'

'Of course not. I'm happy to boost your business any way I can,' he said, surprising himself. Truth was, he wasn't usually a sociable guy, and he never networked at parties. But he was more than happy to help her out, if it meant having her by his side for the rest of the night and keeping that flush of pleasure on her face.

'Well…' She chewed her bottom lip some more. 'That's actually an offer I'm not sure I can afford to refuse…business-wise.'

'Then don't… But let's start with the offer of burnt pig,' he said.

'Absolutely,' she said. 'I'm starving.'

He chuckled at her enthusiastic response, her smoky voice arrowing straight into his groin.

'Cool.' He patted his belly, enjoying the way her gaze tracked down his torso. 'The dancing has made me ravenous, too.'

Although it occurred to him that roast pork wasn't going to satisfy the main reason he was ravenous right now— forcing him to reconsider his priorities again as he led her toward the barbecue pit.

CHAPTER THREE

'I GUESS THAT's my cue to leave,' Charley murmured as the last of the red, white and blue fireworks died in the night sky.

'So soon?' Cade replied, his hand warm on her lower back as he pulled her against him to avoid the couples heading back into the garden.

'It's nearly midnight,' she said, basking in the focussed gaze she had been basking in all evening…the jolt of awareness getting harder and harder to ignore.

Who knew? Cade Landry really was Sir Galahad.

He'd shepherded her around for over two hours, introducing her to female entrepreneurs and businesspeople—as well as a number of wives and girlfriends of the male business people he knew—whose contact details she now had safely secured in her phone. The boost to her business from this evening's networking offensive would be invaluable, and Cade Landry had facilitated it. Even though she'd realised he wasn't much of a social animal. He didn't seem uncomfortable so much as aloof. And from the surprise on a lot of people's faces—including their hosts when Charley had eventually thanked Cassandra in person—she'd gathered he rarely showed at events like this one.

But she had to admit it wasn't her business initiatives she

had been thinking of every time he rested his palm casually on her waist, or smiled that sensual smile full of masculine approval while telling people to check out her dress.

'Which makes it approximately eight in the morning UK time,' she finished, trying to focus on all the reasons why she needed to leave now.

She had a cheap motel booked near the marina which was calling her name. Even though she didn't feel remotely tired, because the giddy excitement of being the sole focus of Cade Landry's attention for the evening had become more than a little addictive.

But Cade hadn't made a move, and she wasn't entirely sure now if she had read his signals all wrong. Was he into her, or was he just being helpful to a fellow businessperson? Because apart from those small, incidental touches, he hadn't made any significant attempts to come on to her since they'd danced their hearts out.

She'd assumed he wanted her...but what did she really know about reading signals? Given that she'd always been so awful at sex? And she hadn't even had any since the first time she'd tried to kiss him...which had been a complete disaster.

'I appreciate everything you've done for me this evening,' she said, her excitement deflating. 'I wouldn't have had the guts to approach most of those people. It was very generous of you. You're actually a nice guy, Sir Galahad,' she teased, covering the flicker of inadequacy.

You don't need his approval, Charley.

His lips twisted in a wry smile. 'The one thing I'm not, Charlotte, is nice,' he said. 'But I made you a promise earlier in the evening, and I never break my word.'

'Okay,' she said, the tension almost as delicious as the sudden spurt of anticipation.

He ran his knuckle down the side of her face. The possessive touch had the endorphins she'd been keeping in check exploding through her system like the fireworks display they'd just witnessed.

'I'd like you to come home with me tonight,' he said, his gaze filling with the molten heat she'd noticed while they danced but had since assumed she must have imagined. The sensual smile made her insides clench. 'But if you're too jet-lagged, or you're just not that into me, I can escort you wherever you want to go.'

'That's…direct,' she whispered, trying desperately not to throw herself at him—something she could acknowledge now she had wanted to do, ever since he had guided her so sensually through the dance. And she'd let him.

That she hadn't read his intentions wrong was even more intoxicating. But something about the insistent pulsing in her sex felt too much like that out-of-control girl.

'Direct is how I roll,' he said. 'When I want something.' He hooked a tendril of hair behind her ear. The casual, oddly possessive gesture made the hunger flare and throb. 'And tonight I want to taste every inch of you and make you moan.' His voice dropped to a husky purr. 'But you need to be sure that's what you want, too.'

It was supposed to be a question. But it didn't sound like one, because her body was already desperate for his touch and had been ever since she'd turned in the garden hours ago to find him watching her…maybe even before that. Maybe even dating right back to that reckless girl who had looked for approval in sex and never found it.

He was the only man who had ever said no to her, she realised—which made his desire for her now all the more exciting. And validating.

'I want you, too' she admitted, because she'd never been coy.

'Thank God,' he said, the scorching heat in his gaze making her realise it had cost him to hold back. 'Then let's get the hell out of here.'

But when he clasped her fingers and strode from the terrace, heading through the house towards the front lawn, the swirl of anticipation in her gut tangled with familiar insecurities.

As they arrived at the valet station and a shiny black SUV appeared, she tugged her hand free.

The sound of the band starting the late-night set floated over the night air but did nothing to calm Charley's nerves. Her life had come full circle since their meeting in Vegas. But it had been years now—four years, to be precise— since she'd been intimate with anyone. And she'd never been any good at it.

'If you've changed your mind, I can take you home,' he said, more perceptive than she would have expected.

'I haven't changed my mind…' she managed around the growing ball of embarrassment wedged in her throat. 'I'm just…'

Good grief, how do you explain to a man who could probably make most women come at thirty paces that you have never had a satisfying sexual experience?

'I'm just not very good at one-night stands…so if you're expecting a sex goddess,' she babbled, 'you're going to be disappointed.'

Rather than looking appalled, Cade's gaze sharpened,

and the heat in his eyes flared. The hot brick between her thighs started to pound.

'Just to be clear, Charlotte.' A confident smile curved his lips. 'No one's going to be grading you on your performance in my bed, either.'

'Good to know,' she mumbled.

Fabulous, Charley. Why not just tell him you're a terrible lay without telling him you're a terrible lay?

'And I happen to be a goal-oriented overachiever who always rises to a challenge,' he added. 'So we're good.'

A laugh burst out of her mouth, his comment so arrogant it somehow managed to be self-deprecating at the same time.

'And let's not forget an ego the size of Pluto,' she said, the knot of embarrassment in her throat releasing.

'Yup,' he said. 'Which, luckily for you, happens to be well-earned.'

She was still chuckling as she climbed into the passenger seat—and the hot, liquid rush of anticipation gushed into her panties.

It was a thirty-minute drive from the Broussards' place to Cade's condo in the Embarcadero. It might as well have taken ten years.

Cade kept his eyes on the road, inhaling Charlotte's intoxicating scent—which had been torturing him all evening—as he wound through the leafy suburbs of Marin County, passed over the Bay on San Francisco's iconic Golden Gate Bridge, then took the 101 through the Presidio, up and down the famous streets of Pacific Heights and Nob Hill and into the built-up areas of downtown. By the time he pulled into the parking garage behind the Ferry Building, the tension in his gut was on a knife edge…

The vintage R&B station he'd found on the radio had done nothing to chill the heat in his gut ever since Charlotte had climbed into his car.

Hell, ever since she'd agreed she wanted him, too. And then told him, with that wary candour, she was no sex goddess—which had to be code for *All the guys I've slept with have been selfish bastards.*

He hadn't lied. He loved a challenge. And he had always been goal-oriented, plus the chemistry between them was nothing short of explosive.

But the hunger which had gripped him ever since they'd danced together had only got worse over the last couple of hours. He had to get a handle on it before he got her naked if he was going to make good on his promise and show her a good time.

He switched off the ignition. Marvin Gaye's sweet soul voice dropped into a charged silence. The heat surged as Charlotte released a careful breath.

'San Francisco is a beautiful city,' she murmured. 'How long have you lived here?'

'I don't,' he said. 'I mostly live in Manhattan, but I keep the condo for when I'm working on the West Coast, because I hate staying in hotels.'

'So do I,' she said. 'It was one of the things I hated the most about modelling. Having my home in a suitcase, being constantly jet-lagged, ordering bar snacks off room service menus because I hadn't eaten all day and that was all I could get at stupid o'clock in the morning. Watching the light blinking on the smoke detector, unable to sleep…' The nervous rush of information cut off abruptly, and she sent him a self-deprecating smile. 'The soulless grind of luxury living has to be the epitome of first-world problems for the spoilt little rich kid I was then, right?'

Her defensiveness, though, told a different story. He'd dismissed her as a spoilt brat that night, just like everyone else, but he could see now it must have been tough getting thrust into that whirlwind when she was still a kid.

'Were you spoilt?' he asked. 'Or just young and unprepared?'

She let out a hollow laugh. 'Who knows.' She shrugged. 'But I'm glad that girl is long gone.' Leaning across the console, she cradled his cheek. 'Are you finally going to kiss me now, Landry?'

He chuckled, the moment of introspection dispelled on a wave of want. Placing his hand on her waist, he dragged her closer and whispered, 'You don't have to ask me again, Charlotte.'

He captured her lips at last. She tasted sultry and sweet. But when her mouth opened on a shocked sob, the kiss went from provocative to carnal in a heartbeat.

He feasted on her, cupping both cheeks, and threading his fingers into her hair to release the soft mass from the chignon which had started to collapse while they danced.

He angled her face, and she opened for him, allowing him to thrust deep and take more. But as she tried to get closer, the seat belt restrained her.

He lifted his head, traced his thumb over her flushed cheek. 'How about we take this upstairs. Making out in a car is overrated.'

'Good plan, Galahad.'

He jumped out and headed round the hood to meet her

at the passenger door. But as she got out, he scooped her into his arms.

She laughed. 'Nice catch.'

She placed eager kisses across his jaw, his chin, his cheek as he marched to the elevator and stabbed the call button with his elbow. The doors opened immediately, but it seemed to take another eternity of torture to finally arrive at his penthouse.

She was still wrapped around him as he walked into the foyer and through into the main living area. The glass walls of the corner penthouse gave him a staggering view of the Bay Bridge and the sprinkle of Oakland's nightlights in the distance, but it wasn't the view which made his breath hitch when he set her on her feet.

She choked out a stuttered sob as he dragged his hands up her thighs under the short mini dress to fill his palms with her soft, responsive and—*what the hell?*—naked butt.

A thong! Lord, help me.

'Were you wearing this the whole time we were dancing?' he accused her, the knife edge becoming painful.

She nodded. 'I love thongs. They're so comfortable.'

He groaned. 'You could have flashed the whole party every time I sent you into a spin...'

'And your point would be...?' She chuckled, giving him a tantalising glimpse of the reckless kid who had once danced on a table.

He laughed too. So the reckless kid wasn't dead and gone—but her bad girl energy was so much more intoxicating now.

Her fingernails rasped across his nape—and sensation arrowed into his groin.

'I think I should punish you,' he murmured, holding her hips. 'For risking getting us both arrested.'

'I agree,' she teased with a throaty purr.

He was still chuckling as he buried his face in her neck to lick the pummelling pulse in her collarbone, while massaging her bare butt and riding his thumb under the string. She shifted, cradling the ridge of his erection against her belly.

He sucked in the musty aroma of her arousal, but then she stiffened.

He pulled back, and saw both giddy need and wary tension in her lust-blown pupils. Small white teeth dug into her bottom lip, making him aware of the reddened skin around her mouth, and on her neck, where he'd given her beard burn.

Slow down, man.

'Hey, are you still with me?' he asked, resting his hand on her neck to stroke the delicate skin with his thumb.

'Yes, yes, of course,' she said too swiftly, as if she was trying to convince herself as well as him. 'I want this,' she added, but she sounded less sure than she had when they'd been devouring each other in the elevator.

He forced himself to loosen his hold a little.

'There's no rush, Charlotte. We can take as long as you need. Tell me where you like to be touched?' he asked, determined to take this at her pace.

She blinked, her eyes dark with arousal, but also wary. Emotion tugged hard under his breastbone.

'Honestly, I'm not sure,' she said. 'No one's ever asked me that before.'

The forthright response was both adorable and kind of sad. He'd bet good money she had lost her virginity long before she'd met him four years ago, but the puzzled frown on her face made her seem like an artless girl—learning about her own desire for the first time.

Right about now, he wanted to murder every guy who had taken from her and given so little back. But the weight of responsibility was also a novel feeling. Could he be the one to show her she had always deserved so much more?

Aware of her nipples standing out like bullet points against the bronze silk, he thumbed one rigid peak. She jolted, her eyes widening.

'How do you like to touch yourself?' he asked, his throat raw as he continued to caress her lazily, not wanting to lose the connection, but careful not to push. 'Can you show me?'

Her pale skin darkened. 'I like what you're doing right now...' she managed. 'But I think it would feel even better if I was naked.'

He let out a strained laugh, the bold comment crucifying him a little.

'Then let's remedy that,' he said.

Gripping the hem of her dress, he drew it gently over her head and threw it away. She quivered, her small, firm breasts barely disguised by red lace.

He found the back hook of her bra, released it. She sighed as he took off the lace. He skimmed his thumb over one ruched nipple. Her vicious shudder rippled through his overwrought body.

Damn, but she was gorgeous. And so responsive...

Lifting the quivering flesh, he dragged his tongue over the swollen peak. She moaned as he drew the hard tip into his mouth and began to suck gently.

She grasped his head and arched her back, instinctively pushing herself into his mouth. Her panting breaths encouraged him as he learned what she liked the most, tormenting and torturing her until the hard peaks elongated even more.

Her musty scent filled his nostrils—sweet and spicy. But he took his time, determined to draw out her pleasure and contain his own—even as her eager, artless responses battered his self-control.

At last, he could wait no longer, cupping her sex, delving beneath the satin shield of her thong. She gasped, so ready and tender each stroke made her buck against his fingers.

He circled the stiff nub, grazing over and around it as he gauged her responses. The pants became sobs, her chest heaving beneath his mouth as he continued to tease her breasts.

'Oh... That's...' She strained against him, her head falling back against the glass wall, the lights of the bay sparkling in her glossy hair.

He lifted his head, blew across her damp nipples, reddened now from his attention, and continued to work her clitoris with his thumb. He pressed one finger, then two inside her—his breathing becoming ragged at the realisation of how tight and wet she was. For him.

'Relax, Charlotte, and let it take you...' he coaxed, focussing his caresses on the slick heart of her at last.

She jerked, bucked against him, her hands grasping fistfuls of his shirt as she shuddered through the climax—the tortured sounds she made part pleasure, part pain.

Her body sank against the glass as the orgasm ebbed. He withdrew his hand, rested it on her hip. And waited for her eyes to open.

The green gaze locked on his, her expression dazed. Something pure and strong cinched tight around his ribs.

She seemed fragile and strangely vulnerable in that moment—her hair a soft, tangled mess, her breasts reddened from his lips, her sultry fragrance filling the room, and her face unable to hide her astonishment. As if the bad girl had been stripped away to reveal the needy, neglected girl beneath.

'How…how did you do that?' she asked, perplexed. 'I've never… Well…'

The swell of affection and pride—because he had given her something precious—made his lungs tighten. How could she be so bold, jaded even…and yet also so unsure?

She was much more complex and fascinating than he could have imagined.

'It's not hard to pay attention…' he said, then pressed his palm to her flushed skin. 'How do you feel about another round?'

The chance to explore all those facets, unravel more of the puzzle she represented, excited him beyond bearing.

It occurred to him he'd become impossibly jaded about sex too, because her unguarded response to each touch, each caress, was somehow more erotic than the most practised seductress.

A grin split her features. 'Much more enthusiastic now.'

Gripping his shoulders, she leapt into his arms—the reckless girl returning. He caught her with a huff, his hands gravitating to her backside.

'But I want you naked too, Galahad.'

'No problem,' he said, enjoying her demanding tone.

He strode into the master suite and dropped her on the bed, then ripped open his shirt.

Her eyes flared with excitement as she watched him strip.

'What's the tattoo on your shoulder?' she asked.

He paused as her avid gaze roamed over the ink he'd got at seventeen to celebrate flipping his first house—a broken-down two-storey Arcadian in Breaux Bridge, Louisiana, which he'd gutted and remodelled over one endless, back-breaking summer.

'A phoenix,' he said, embarrassed by the dumb decision now, made when he'd been drunk with excitement about the big fat profit burning a hole in his wallet. 'Kind of a cliché, but it seemed appropriate at the time,' he added, because he'd come to despise that ink in some ways, and the naive kid who had thought he'd be accepted, just because he had money to invest.

'It's cool,' she said as she kicked off the ankle boots she still wore. 'And very hot!'

He smiled. Maybe that decision hadn't been so dumb after all?

He ripped open his pants, shoved them down. But as his erection bounced free, thick and long and impossibly hard, surprise flared across her features.

'That's impressive,' she said, the bold tone husky with desire, but also unsure again.

He'd had compliments before about his physique—he was a man who women had always liked the look of, even when he'd been broke—but something about the stunned yearning in her gaze when it rose to his, the captivating mix of awareness and shock, had him feeling like a real knight in shining armour for the first time in his life.

A knight who planned to show Charlotte Courtney exactly what she had been missing.

Cade Landry is actually a sex god!

Excitement vibrated in Charley's gut as she devoured

the sight of Cade's heavily muscled body—in all its naked glory. The small scars, the flamboyant tattoo in faded red and gold of the mythical bird flaming across his left pec and shoulder, the defined lines of his hip flexors, the washboard abs, and the sunburnt bronze of his skin which paled at his groin, framing the massive erection that jutted out from the nest of dark hair.

She swallowed around the new blockage in her throat. And stared.

But as he fished a condom out of the bedside dresser and rolled it onto the mammoth erection with casual efficiency, it occurred to her he was a lot more experienced at pleasuring women than she was at pleasuring a man.

And she'd never had any satisfaction at all from penetrative sex.

The truth was, all her sexual encounters up to now had been furtive and rushed, crude and unmemorable...

She forced herself not to tense up, tried to concentrate on the epic orgasm she'd just had—which had been as surprising as it had been exhilarating.

Cade had taken his own sweet time and devoted himself to her pleasure first and foremost. Which just went to show, the few guys she'd slept with before him had been incredibly selfish, dating right back to the forty-something photographer who had slammed into her in a studio bathroom when she was sixteen and convinced her it was her fault she hadn't enjoyed it.

She wanted to believe she'd just turned a corner—with Cade Landry's expert help. But as he climbed onto the bed and gripped her ankle to tug her towards him—fierce possession in his eyes—her breath hitched. She did not want this to be another encounter she ended up regretting.

She pressed a hand to his chest. 'Wait.'

'Problem?' he asked, his hands stroking her hips in a way which made her heart thunder against her ribs.

'Not specifically...' she said, far too aware of the thrusting flesh brushing against her thigh. Being in that state had to be uncomfortable, but in her experience, men found it a lot harder to slow down once they got it inside you.

'I just... I don't want this to be over too soon.' She gripped the hot length as carefully as she could. 'So how about I take care of you?'

He jolted as she stroked the turgid flesh, but then he pressed a kiss to her cheek and grasped her wrist to remove her hand from the powerful erection.

'I'm in no rush, Charlotte,' he said, the amusement in his voice belied by the intensity in his expression. 'Let's make this all about you. Because believe me, I'm already being taken care of...'

'You *are*?' she asked. But she felt gauche and insecure when he chuckled.

'Do you have any idea how captivating you are?' he countered without answering her inane question. Before she could come up with a coherent answer, he murmured, 'How about I show you...'

It wasn't a question, as he held her firmly in place to nuzzle her neck, then proceeded to kiss his way—with infuriating patience—down her torso.

He worshipped her with his mouth, his tongue, his teeth. His lazy focus made her aware of each sweet, sensitive spot he discovered. The maddeningly slow caresses turned her collarbone, her breasts, her nipples, her belly into one enormous erogenous zone. Her back bowed as he awakened every nerve ending—building a new maelstrom of need. She grasped handfuls of the sheet as he finally blew across the soaked satin of her thong.

She gasped, desperate, devastated as he traced the edge with his tongue.

'Please…take it off…' she begged, the thin swatch of fabric a frustrating barrier.

'Why yes, Mizz Charlotte,' he teased, the husky edge in his voice vibrating against her skin before he eased the thong off.

She lay hesitant, expectant, the mix of brutal pleasure and vicious anticipation making her desperation increase, as he parted her swollen folds and lathed his tongue across the needy flesh.

She lurched off the bed, her fingers fisting in the luxury linen sheets again, her eyes screwed shut.

'Easy, Charlotte, hold on to it this time,' he murmured, the tone arrogant but full of a confidence which only made her feel more alive, more needy, and more secure. And very happy to let him lead. 'We've got all night.'

She parted her thighs, brushed the silky waves of his hair she could reach with her fingertips to urge him on, as he went to work, devouring her with his tongue, but retreating every time she edged too close to another glorious release.

Pleasure swelled and twisted—taut, tight, painful—building her desperation.

The wave barrelled towards her just as he rose above her, his broad shoulders cutting out the night.

Clasping her hips, spreading her wide, he surged deep in one powerful, all-consuming thrust. The thick erection stretched her unbearably, but her body was so slick, so ready, he impaled her with ease.

She sobbed, shocked by how the thick intrusion made

the climax intensify. He established an undulating, unstop-pable rhythm and forced her to follow, reminding her of the dance. She clung to him again, trusting him to show her the way.

She dug her heels into the mattress, her knees gripping his hips, and rode the brutal wave, which rose to crest again as he pounded into her, the pleasure so much, too much… much more than enough.

She cried out, her voice hoarse, as she dived into the hot vat of stunning sensation.

'Look at me,' he growled, his tone raw.

Her eyelids flew open, and she found him watching her with that fierce intensity—but he was lost now too in the maddening pleasure… His movements became jerky and frantic. His gruff shout of completion pierced the thick fog of afterglow.

Triumph filled her—sweet, visceral, overwhelming—as he collapsed on top of her, following her head first into the abyss…

CHAPTER FOUR

WELL... HELL...

Cade eased out of Charlotte's body and flopped onto his back on the bed—exhausted, drained, and still tingling with the power of his orgasm.

She moved beside him, her breathing as uneven and unsteady as his.

He managed to turn his head and caught her staring back at him. Her lust-blown pupils and the flushed glow on her skin both a validation and a warning.

Had she felt it too? The intensity of their connection? Because he'd never experienced anything like it before. And he'd slept with a lot of women—maybe not as many as his reputation on social media suggested, but enough to know that had been spectacular. And he was not a guy given to hyperbole.

A smile edged her lips, her expression more open than he had ever seen it, making her seem artless—and impossibly young.

'Thank you, Sir Galahad,' she said, her gaze unguarded. 'Finally I know what all the fuss is about.'

He forced out a gruff laugh.

'You're welcome, Mizz Charlotte,' he said, trying to lift the weight pressing on his chest.

They'd been waiting to explore their chemistry for hours. And he didn't do deferred gratification, if he could help it... Plus it had been a month since he'd had any sex at all. And a whole lot longer since he'd slept with a woman as captivating as Charlotte Courtney.

But what they had shared was still only sex. Ultimately, this hookup was no different to all the others. It couldn't be.

She yawned and let out a throaty sigh, which had the heat in his groin pulsing.

Seriously? How could he want her again so soon after that mind-blowing orgasm?

But then she dragged herself off the bed and began rooting around for her clothes.

He propped himself up on his elbow. 'What are you doing? It's two in the morning.'

She glanced over her shoulder, having slipped on the thong, flashing him a delicious view of her rear end.

'Heading back to my motel before I drop into a coma,' she said. 'I haven't slept for close to twenty-four hours now, and I'm out of practice doing all-nighters.'

Surprise was followed by disappointment. He wasn't ready for her to leave. Another first.

'Come back to bed,' he said, grabbing his shorts and tugging them on to cross the room. He lifted the silk dress out of her hands before she could slip it over her head. 'Sleep here.'

'Won't that get weird?' she asked with her usual directness. 'Tomorrow morning?'

He brushed her hair back to hook the unruly curls behind her ear, captivated all over again, and he wasn't even sure why. She wasn't wrong. He wasn't a snuggler—once sex was done, he preferred to sleep alone—and mornings after could be just plain awkward, if his latest hookup had expectations of anything more substantial. But somehow, with Charlotte, he doubted that would be a problem.

And weirdly, her reluctance only made him more determined to get her to stay.

'Why would it be weird?' he asked to delay her.

She shrugged. 'Walk of shame-wise? You really have to ask?'

'I'm not ashamed of what just happened,' he countered. 'Are you?'

'No, of course not,' she said, but a hot rush of colour suffused her features.

He pressed a kiss to her forehead, feeling strangely protective of her. As a kid she'd been left to fend for herself in a very adult world. No wonder she was wary of being caught leaving his place. After the *Blush* piece—and the viral storm still raging online—he knew what it felt like now to be objectified by social media's keyboard warriors.

'How about I help you to leave incognito tomorrow?' he said. 'The people hounding me on social media aren't aware I'm in San Francisco yet.' Or he certainly hoped they weren't.

He'd like to see her again, but he could take his time if no one found out what had happened tonight. Luke's party was famous for its privacy. And they hadn't been seen anywhere public. So they were both good.

But why not make Charlotte his summer date after all? They'd have to figure out some stuff—logistics-wise—because she lived in London. And her brother might pitch a fit—but it would be worth the extra effort. One thing was for damn sure, he didn't see himself getting bored with her soon.

She looked at him for the longest time, the flush on her pearly skin intensifying. His insides clenched. The desire for her to stay overnight and be here in the morning was unprecedented. And did not have one damn thing to do with the bet, if he were being honest.

Then her face broke into a huge yawn.

'Come on.' He took her hand, drew her toward the bed.

Throwing back the sheet, he guided her in, then climbed in to drag her body against his. Spooning for the first time in his life.

His body responded accordingly.

She shifted against him. 'FYI, I'm far too shattered to do anything about that…'

He smiled against her hair, his arm tightening around her waist. 'Ignore it. It'll go down eventually.'

Although it took a while, because listening to her breathing deepen was impossibly arousing, too.

He stared out into the San Francisco night, his body pounding with need, and wondered when and how he had become so enchanted by her.

But as he drifted into sleep himself, finally letting the hunger go, he persuaded himself his desire to keep Charlotte for longer than he'd originally planned was all about finding a way to win the bet…while also having an entertaining and enjoyable summer.

No big deal.

CHAPTER FIVE

CHARLEY'S EYES FLUTTERED open to find her nose pushed into firm tanned flesh which smelled of salt and pine woods and man.

Mmm... Delicious.

But then full consciousness returned.

Cade Landry!

She was wrapped around the man she had spent one incredible night with at Cassandra Broussard's party. But the awareness making all her pulse points pound was soon joined by a wave of panic.

She shifted away from him, her disorientated senses becoming aware not just of all the places her body felt different—well-used, a little sore—but also that the night had meant more to her than it should.

Why else was she still in his bed? She had never spent the whole night with a guy.

She could remember the stunning orgasms, him coaxing her to stay, the promise to help her leave this morning in secret—and her insistence staying was a bad idea. So why had she succumbed?

Jet lag? Maybe. Exhaustion? Possibly.

But even as she tried to convince herself there were lots

of practical reasons for her to fall asleep in Cade's bed, the panic in her chest became a ticking bomb.

Stop analysing your stupidity and get out of here—now.

Galvanised, she edged off the bed. He lay, still fast asleep, taking up most of the available space. She stared at him for one precious moment. Weren't guys supposed to look boyish and less threatening and overpowering while asleep?

Trust Cade Landry to be the opposite. His hard, handsome face—the stubble on his jaw almost a beard now—was even more devastating. Serious and hot, and totally intimidating.

The ticking time bomb pushed into her throat as she recalled how careful, how intent he had been on her pleasure, her response to him.

No man had ever made love to her with such focus.

Not made love...had sex.

He'd said himself it was no big deal. All he'd had to do was pay attention. She'd obviously just picked the wrong guys to get intimate with before Cade.

No biggie.

He frowned in his sleep, shifting. And she jerked back.

She scrambled off the bed, her heart now pressed against her larynx.

She gathered her discarded clothing and slipped each piece on—from her signature dress, now hopelessly crushed, to the tangled thong.

As she yanked on her ankle boots, she became brutally aware of the discomfort between her thighs, the tenderness in her sex. She needed a shower. But she wasn't about to risk waking him, the ticking bomb threatening to explode.

Her flight home was booked for three o'clock. She had

enough time to catch a cab back to her motel in Marin
County, grab a shower and her luggage, then head to the
airport.

She paused while scooping up the purse she'd dropped
in the living room.

The penthouse's panoramic view of the Bay Bridge and
the heritage building in front of them—ornate and dazzling in the sunlight—had the breath she'd been holding
clogging her lungs.

The memory of the approval in Cade's eyes all through
the evening and during their night together—as he'd played
her body like a virtuoso, and she'd enjoyed every minute
of it—filled her with a fierce yearning which only made
her feel more exposed. And frankly idiotic.

Orgasms were one thing. Even breathtaking, life-al-
tering, mind-blowing ones. But the fact Cade had been
the man to deliver them—a man who in a weird way had
changed the course of her life four years ago—felt significant. But she refused to be one of those women who
confused great sex and electrifying chemistry with something more.

She turned from the magnificent view and spotted a
notepad on the coffee table.

She jotted down a quick note. Then screwed it up and
stuffed it in her purse. It took two more attempts before she
got the right mix of friendly and flippant.

As she walked through the parking area ten minutes
later, she refused to acknowledge the regret making her
chest ache.

She was not that needy, messed-up girl any more.

This wasn't a walk of shame. She didn't care if her make-
up was smudged, her dress wrinkled and her scent more

than a little musty. She was one hundred percent respon-
sible for her actions last night. And she'd had a good time.
An illuminating time.

But she would shove this memory away in a box marked
'Your First Booty Call to Remember' and then forget about
Cade, finally, because she'd come full circle from the reck-
less girl he'd met four years ago.

And she had no doubt at all, Cade Landry would be
grateful when he woke up to discover she had taken the
initiative—and left before things could get awkward.

*Thanks for an epic night, Sir Galahad! If I ever get the
chance to dance the Zydeco again, I'll think of you. C*

Cade stared at the note—which he'd found propped on the
coffee table after spending ten minutes searching the apartment for his overnight guest.

Her sultry perfume had woken him from vivid erotic
dreams—in which she was the star player, his groin hard
and throbbing. And now *this*…

She'd run out on him.

He scratched his stomach, still groggy and strung out
after the deepest sleep he'd had in months, and read the
note again.

The blip in his heartbeat, though, refused to subside. But
as he scanned the note a third time, looking for any kind of
hidden meaning, any hint she planned to get in touch with
him again, anger tangled with the hollow ache in his gut.

She hadn't even left a cell number. This was the female
equivalent of *wham, bam, thank you, ma'am.*

He'd been given the kiss-off before—back in high
school, when the rich, pretty, popular girls had been happy

to use him for kicks but had never wanted to date him in public—and it had stopped bothering him a long time ago.

So why did Charlotte Courtney's kiss-off note bug him so much now?

Perhaps because he thought he'd left that easily used kid behind after he'd made his first million. Perhaps because these days, he was always the one to disengage first. Maybe even because he'd decided late last night that Charlotte would be the perfect summer date to see off deMarco and her brother when it came to the Helberg bet?

But as he screwed up the note and lobbed it into the trash, determined to forget it, and her—Charlotte's breezy, brazen, couldn't-give-a-damn-about-you note still bugged him. Big-time.

What the hell had he expected? Yeah, it had been a memorable night, one of the best he'd had in a while. But that was as much to do with the fact he'd been working his nuts off for months, preparing the groundwork to bring Helberg and its assets into the Landry brand, as it did with Charlotte.

As for making her his summer date? He could always find someone else…

They hadn't arrived at the Broussards' together, and the press had been long gone by the time they'd left. No one knew about last-night's hook up, so his options were still open.

It was all good. Or at least it ought to be…

But after showering and changing, he gave in to the urge to contact his cleaning crew, to ensure they put fresh linens on the bed so he wouldn't be able to smell Charlotte when he returned that evening. Which was more than a bit obsessive—because they didn't need reminding to change his sheets.

As he headed out for a series of meetings with his architects—to discuss plans for one of Helberg's old hotels in the Presidio—he couldn't shake the hollow ache in his chest. Or the constant blip in his heart rate...

While he spent the day discussing the cost and scope of the renovation work needed, thoughts of Charlotte—so captivating, so fierce, so forthright and alive as she discovered the joys of Zydeco and sex—kept intruding and making him lose the thread of the conversation.

By the time he got back to the apartment that night, he was exhausted and still preoccupied with every damn detail of what had happened between them—which wasn't like him at all.

He'd never had trouble moving on before, even back in high school.

But he couldn't shift the unpleasant thought that something had slipped through his fingers, something he wanted and couldn't have. Something he hadn't even known he wanted until he'd met Charlotte Courtney again—and danced with her in the moonlight.

He wasn't that reject kid any more who allowed other people to call the shots or let himself be hurt because people thought they were better than him.

So why had he let Charlotte's crummy kiss-off note make him feel like that again?

Damn her.

CHAPTER SIX

One week later

'HI, CHARLEY. I'VE asked our photographer, Rapinda, to send you some shots from our Fourth of July event.' Cassandra Broussard's voice was warm and friendly on the other end of the transatlantic phone line. 'The ones of you in your dress are terrific, definitely something to use on your social media channels.'

'Wow, really? Thank you so much, Cassie.' Charley beamed as she took in the view from the new space she was hoping to rent for Trouble Maker Designs, overlooking Shoreditch High Street. The elevated overground train line and the market stalls below gave the space a funky urban setting which was perfect for her brand. The bright, airy offices of an old printing warehouse also gave her the space she needed to hire some seamstresses. Working out of her front room wasn't going to cut it any more. 'I've had four commissions already from the connections I made at your party. I really can't thank you enough.'

Her new best friend gave an easy laugh. 'My pleasure, Charley. We don't usually issue photos from the event to the media, but Luke agreed the shots of you and Cade Landry were too good to waste. You guys look fabulous together.'

'Right. Thanks,' Charley said, her excitement downgrading at the mention of the man she hadn't been able to stop thinking about for over a week. 'It was fun,' she added.

Too much fun, really. Because she hadn't been able to stop second-guessing her decision to run out on Cade ever since.

If only she could start sleeping again, without dreaming about his hands, his lips, his tongue inciting her senses, the wry sensual smile curving his lips, or the tattoo on his chest tensing as he came with a throaty roar...

Heat exploded across her collarbone.

Yes, if only...

'Okay, well, my work here is done,' Cassie said, thankfully not asking any awkward questions about Cade.

As soon as the call ended, Charley checked her in-box and found a link to a file-sharing site. After pressing Download, ten photos flashed onto her phone.

As she examined each one, her heartbeat slowed, and heat burned her cheeks.

Rapinda Patel was clearly another of Cassie's protégés, because her work was exquisite, the shots vibrant and yet so fresh and real, capturing her and Cade in sharp focus on the dance floor—amidst a blur of colour.

Her bronze silk minidress looked incredible—sultry and sophisticated, but also fun and flirty. It made a statement about the Trouble Maker brand which Charley couldn't have replicated even if she'd paid a fortune for studio shots... But it was the two of them together—Cade's striking handsomeness, the strength of his body, the rugged appreciation in his expression and the fierce joy on her face as he launched her into a twirl—which made the biggest impression, adding raw sex appeal and dreamy romance to the compositions.

She let out a slow breath. She had to use them.

Surely he wouldn't care? It was a tiny bit dodgy to use his image without his consent. But contacting him was out of the question… He might think she hadn't moved on the way he had, and hearing that low, sexy Southern accent again would not help with her sleep deprivation.

She swallowed down the foolish yearning making her chest ache…just a little.

You made the right choice, Charley. Time to concentrate on your business now, instead of a one-night stand that didn't mean anything…

Decision made, she framed her three favourite shots, opened all the Trouble Maker accounts on the different apps she used, wrote a quick caption, and launched the stunning shots onto the internet before she could start the second-guessing game again.

Confidence and excitement—and a strange breathlessness—washed away the prickle of unease as likes started popping up seconds later.

Cassie Broussard had given her the shots to use. And what would be the point of going to the most exclusive event of the summer season in the US if she couldn't take the best advantage of it?

Anyway, she needed the confidence boost, because she had to ring her brother Adam now…and beg him to release fifty thousand pounds from the trust fund her mother had left her that he still controlled. She'd made a point of never dipping into it before. Partly because she wanted to succeed on her own terms, but mostly because she had got the hump when she'd asked Adam for some start-up funding after graduating from fashion college and he had insisted she write a business plan. If that wasn't code for 'I don't trust you to make smart, career-focussed decisions and not muck this up', she did not know what was. She'd decided to use her own savings from her catwalk days to get started.

But she couldn't possibly handle all the commissions she already had on her own. So she was going to have to suck up her pride and persuade Adam she was a good investment. Maybe she didn't have a business plan which would impress him—she wasn't the CEO of a Fortune 500 company, after all—but she knew what she wanted, she knew the fashion business, and she had verifiable proof now her designs were good enough to attract the clientele she needed to turn Trouble Maker into a success.

End of.

Even so, her palms were sweating as she switched off the whirlwind of notifications on her phone and dailed Adam's private number. It was six in the morning Manhattan time, but Adam always woke up before dawn because he was a total workaholic—when he wasn't being a One Date Wonder.

As expected, her brother picked up on the second ring—sounding alert and aloof and as if he had shaved and showered and probably taken a five-mile run already.

'Charley, is there a problem?' he said without a hello.

She sighed. 'No! Why do you always assume there's a problem that you need to fix when I call you?'

'Because there usually is,' he said far too patiently. 'I distinctly recall getting a call at five a.m. when you had to be bailed out of a cell in Barcelona for swearing at a police officer.'

'That was years ago. And I didn't swear at him. It was a translation problem.'

'Or the time you ran away from St Jude's and wanted train fare to get to London.'

'That is actually ancient history.'

'The point is, Charley, you never phone me unless there's a problem. I always phone you.'

'Okay, fair point.' She bit down on the urge to point out she had been the one to phone once, begging to come back home after their father had sent her off to boarding school. But Adam hadn't been interested in talking about those messy things called emotions at the time. And now she was positive he only rang her out of a sense of duty and to check she wasn't still making a mess of her life. But she had to ask him a favour, so buttoning her resentment was necessary.

All part of being a grown-up businesswoman and not a screwed-up wild child.

'So why *are* you calling?' he asked bluntly. Adam didn't really do small talk any more than Cade Landry.

Then a thought occurred to her, a way of easing into the conversation about trust funds and business initiatives.

'I thought you'd like to know I was at tech billionaire Luke Broussard's Fourth of July bash in Marin County last weekend. The photos I just posted of me wearing one of my designs are already going viral, which is going to be invaluable publicity for Trouble Maker. *Free* publicity. *Organic* publicity. Plus, I picked up four new commissions while I was there. So I've decided to expand my operation...'

'Let me take a look,' he cut in, using the authoritative tone he always used when they spoke about her business—

as if he was the only person in the world who knew how to run one efficiently.

'I posted them on all the Trouble Maker accounts,' she murmured, although the silence suggested he wasn't listening while he loaded them onto his phone.

A prickle of unease worked its way up her neck and then slithered down her spine as she imagined her brother examining the shots of her and Cade Landry dancing together... Surely he wouldn't be able to tell they'd done a lot more than just dance?

'Is that Cade Landry?' he asked, the interest in his tone surprising her. Adam never asked about her social life. Usually because it would mean talking about his own.

'Yes, I... Do you know him?' Heat scalded her cheeks.

'We play squash occasionally,' he murmured, obviously still examining the photos of them dancing in minute detail. 'How do *you* know him?'

Terrific. Why hadn't she guessed her brother would know the man she'd had a torrid one-night stand with? Of course he would. Her luck was just that good.

She was still struggling to come up with an answer—which didn't sound like a lie—when Adam added, 'Because you seem extremely...close.'

'Stop looking at Cade and me and look at the dress!' she replied, exasperated and desperate to deflect the conversation before she spontaneously combusted from embarrassment. 'The point is those photos have already got a lot of views and...'

'Damn it, Charley, please tell me you didn't sleep with the guy.' The frustrated comment came so out of left field—because she and Adam *never* talked about anything *that* personal—the knee-jerk response was out of her mouth before she could consider how much it revealed.

'And that would be your business, why, exactly?'

He swore on the other end of the line. 'He's a player and a loner and is not good relationship material…'

'I'm not that naive, Adam,' she said, oddly intrigued by Adam's insight into Cade Landry's character. She'd guessed Cade was a loner at the party, but why did it suddenly seem significant?

'He's also in the market to acquire Helberg Holdings,' Adam continued.

'So what?' She knew Adam was after Helberg because their father had sold their mother's much-loved jewellery business, Montague's, to Reed Helberg for a single dollar out of spite. Although she'd never quite figured out why Adam was so hung up about buying it back again. Their mother had died fourteen years ago. But then, Charley had never presumed to understand her brother's motives for doing anything. She suspected it had something to do with the focussed and controlled and extremely dull person he'd become after their mother's suicide. But then Adam had been much closer to their mother than Charley had, probably because he'd had a chance to know her before her mental health had been so fragile and she'd become disconnected from reality.

But what did any of that have to do with her and Cade?

'So, I made a bet with him and Zane,' he said, sounding almost hesitant—not like him at all. 'Which you're now mixed up in.'

'What bet?'

The long-suffering sigh was new, too. When was the last

time Adam had struggled to talk down to her, or explain in a patronising way what she needed to do next...?

'It was thought to be a good way to decide who should have Helberg without driving up the share price.'

'Adam, would you please get to the point. What bet did you make with Cade, and how could it possibly involve me?' Because that made no sense whatsoever... Adam had no idea she and Cade had ever met before their night together a week ago.

'We only date one woman for the duration of the summer, until Labor Day.'

What the...?

'Are you serious?' she murmured.

But before she could even acknowledge exactly how crass their bet was, between three grown men for goodness' sake, Adam replied.

'Unfortunately, yes, I wouldn't joke about anything that involves Montague's. I suspect he hit on you to provoke me.'

Her blood went cold, the humiliation she'd felt once before in connection with Cade Landry dowsing her like a bucket of ice water...

She hadn't just slept with Cade. She'd had the best sex of her life with him. And she thought they'd connected on some emotional level. He'd made her feel seen, feel cherished, feel important—and all the time he'd only picked her to have a go at her brother? And to win a bet?

The bastard.

'How did you get those photos?' Adam asked. 'The party was over a week ago.'

'Why is that significant?' she said, her chest still imploding with mortification.

'He hasn't been seen dating anyone yet in public. But

now those pictures are going viral, he's going to have to stick with you. Unless I'm overreacting and he *didn't* intend for you to be the one woman.'

Adam's reasoning didn't make her feel any better. In fact, it made her feel much worse. Cade had slept with her and then decided, *what*? That she wasn't someone he wanted to date for the whole summer? No wonder he'd offered to usher her out of the building incognito the next morning.

The absolute bastard.

And she'd now messed with his plan by publishing those photos.

Well, good.

Now he wouldn't be able to date anyone else for the rest of the summer. She hoped he died of sexual frustration. She let the anger in to fill up the empty space inside her—the empty space she remembered only too well.

Because it had always been there. Every time her mother looked right through her as a little girl. Or every time her father refused to be moved by her grief, or her unhappiness, or the reckless bad behaviour she'd resorted to as a teenager to get his attention. Or every time Adam had been condescending or patronising as a way not to engage with who she was as a person.

What a fool she'd been to think for a moment the night she and Cade had shared, the connection they'd made, had been real.

'Fine, well,' she said, feeling broken again, in a way she hadn't in four years. 'That makes me feel so much better. *Not*.'

'I'll fix it,' said Adam, as if this was somehow his problem, when she knew it was all hers.

'No, *I'll* fix it,' she replied.

'I'm sorry. I did not mean for you to get caught in the middle of all this,' Adam began.

'I need you to release fifty thousand pounds from my trust fund.' She sliced neatly into his mea culpa, desperate to change the subject before the last of her confidence got flushed down the toilet. 'I can send you the contract for the space I'm planning to rent and the projections for the equipment and staff I need to hire to get my new commissions out...'

Perhaps there could be an upside to how devastated and humiliated she felt right now? The grinding pain in her stomach a reminder never to trust rich, entitled men who danced like gods and knew how to make you beg.

'That's why I was *actually* calling you...' she finished.

Not to have a debate about my recent dating history, which has made me feel like crap.

'I'll speak to the bank and have them release the funds,' Adam said without an argument—which meant he had to be feeling really guilty.

Unfortunately, though, it wasn't Adam she wanted to punch in the gut.

'Send over your projections,' he said, morphing into CEO mode, which was his default. 'I'll check them over and...'

'Thanks Adam, will do,' she said and disconnected the call. Before he could say more.

She needed to breathe, to ease the grinding pain in her stomach.

But as the pain twisted and tightened into hard, greasy knots, the idea of the new warehouse space she would now have the money to rent didn't fill her with the joy it had twenty minutes ago.

Had Cade Landry soured that, too?

She hated that he'd got to her. That she had liked him. That it had been more to her than sex, even though she'd spent a week trying to convince herself otherwise.

She considered deleting the photos of them together on the internet, because they were horribly tarnished now, too. Not a bright, beautiful moment of romance and possibilities and raw vivid sexuality, but a testament to what a fool she'd been to believe, for even a second, he'd seen more in her than just an easy conquest.

But as the likes and reposts and notifications continued to mount during the day, she began to relish the opportunity to get the word out about her business. When she started getting calls from journalists, she fielded the ones about her 'exciting new romance' with Cade by neither confirming or denying they were an item, stoking the media storm deliberately.

Why should she have any qualms about using the so-called 'Latest It Couple Romance' between the One Date Wonder Billionaire and the Former British Wild Child Turned Fashion Sensation to publicise Trouble Maker—when he'd had no qualms about using her?

A text arrived a few hours later from a withheld number. It simply said,

Charlotte, we need to talk…

She blocked the number, then booked the three-week buying trip to Italy which she had been planning for months to source fabrics for her designs. She could work on the designs for her new commissions from a base in Lake Como—the heart of Italian silk manufacture—while also visiting factories she'd short-listed in Tuscany and Puglia for the best wool and cotton producers.

Completely coincidentally, it would keep her out of London until the celebrity gossip mill had run its course.

Of course, her absence would also make it impossible for Cade Landry to contact her, which was just as well, because she never intended to see or speak to that rat bastard ever again.

CHAPTER SEVEN

Three weeks later

AS THE LANDRY chopper settled onto the lawn of the lavish belle époque villa hotel on the banks of Lake Como, Cade could feel the fury and frustration he had been holding in check for weeks start to choke him.

The hotel's staff rushed to meet him. Not surprising, given Landry Construction had spent a small fortune booking out every single room. Alongside the staff was the detective he'd hired—when Charlotte Courtney had hurled him into the middle of a social media tornado, then blocked his calls and disappeared.

As soon as the detective had contacted his PA with her whereabouts, he'd taken the company jet to Italy—more than ready to give her one hell of a nasty surprise.

'Clear to disembark,' the pilot announced.

After ripping off his headphones, Cade strode from the big black bird to be greeted by the young female investigator.

'Where is she?' he shouted above the thunder from slowing the blades.

'I can take you to her, *signor*. She is at a silk factory fifteen minutes' drive from this location.'

'No.' The last thing he needed was for them to get caught in public having a catfight.

Because he had no doubt Charlotte was not going to agree to what had to happen next without an argument. Her outspoken behaviour had captivated him in San Francisco. All it did now was infuriate him.

The prickle of awareness at the thought of seeing her again—and forcing her to return to the US with him—called him a liar. He dismissed it, because his libido and their combustible chemistry were not the driving force behind this situation any more.

The woman was a reckless, impulsive nightmare. But she'd left him with no choice. They were going to have to be a couple for the rest of the summer if he was going to win Helberg—a direct result of her decision to post those damn photos without asking him first.

The helicopter lifted into the sky and disappeared across the lake.

The approaching twilight gave the water a golden glow. The four-storey Italianate villa nestled into terraced botanical gardens which now housed a five-star hotel and spa couldn't have looked more romantic.

Cade frowned. *How damned ironic.*

But the estate was also situated at the end of a private road. After spending a day moving the guests out at his request, the management had been more than willing to accommodate his meeting with Charlotte in complete privacy.

There would be no photographers, no press, and no members of the public to interrupt them—or witness any temper tantrums—while he explained to her in words of one syllable the consequences of her actions.

She'd got her pound of flesh—using his image to push

her business. Now she was going to have to deal with the fallout—just like he'd been dealing with it for three solid weeks.

'She's going to be here tonight?' he asked as they headed across the manicured lawn. 'And she doesn't know I'll be here?'

The detective nodded. 'Yes, her driver and the *agriturismo* where she has been staying have been generously compensated for their cooperation.'

Cade nodded. It had been a major operation—and cost a small fortune—but no way was he giving her the chance to run out on him again.

The hotel manager arrived to greet them both as Cade and the detective walked into the hotel's grandiose foyer.

'We have *la terrazza privata* ready for your evening meal, Signor Landry, as soon as your guest arrives,' the hotel's executive manager said with a confident smile. 'It is *bellissima* in the sunset, perfect for *un appuntamento romantico.*'

A romantic date, my ass.

Cade's Italian didn't have to be fluent for him to guess even the middle-aged Italian hotel boss had probably heard of the media furore surrounding his 'romance' with Charlotte—which had only started to calm down in the last week.

Great.

The inconvenient prickle of awareness became a definite hum as he headed up to the penthouse suite and showered off the twelve-hour flight.

The fury and frustration which had been driving him for weeks—every time he got doorstepped by another celebrity hack, every time his team hit another dead end while trying to locate Charlotte, every time he relived the moment when he had woken up alone in his Embarcadero apartment and found her damn kiss-off note—finally began to ease. In its place, anticipation and something which felt a lot like exhilaration surged. As the sun sank towards the lake, he imagined the not so *romantico* date he had planned for this evening's entertainment, once he finally had Charlotte back where he wanted her.

'Carlo, dov'é questo?' Charley asked the local driver she'd hired as the cab wound down the poplar-flanked driveway of an extremely expensive lakeside estate.

Carlo had told her—from what she could gather with her rusty Italian—that Signor Chiesa, the farmer she'd been staying with for two weeks, had arranged alternative accommodation for her tonight because of a broken *something* at his farm. But this couldn't be right? It looked way outside her budget.

'Non posso pagare,' she added, trying to explain she couldn't pay for this place.

'Si, si, é tutto pagato,' Carlo replied.

It was all paid for... *Really?*

Her eyes widened as the cab drove out of the trees and a magnificent villa appeared, situated in palatial gardens on the edge of the lake. The historic structure's ornate plasterwork and lavish design were a testament to a bygone era of nineteenth-century grandeur. It looked more like a royal palace than a hotel, despite the discreet sign announcing it as La Bella Grande Villa Hotel.

Charley was still staring at the luxurious building as she stepped out of the car.

She asked again—in her broken Italian—if Carlo was sure this was the right place.

But he simply smiled and nodded, then handed her the precious case full of samples she'd spent the day collecting before firing off some fatherly advice about getting a good night's rest. She was still standing there, dwarfed by the magnificent hotel, as she watched Carlo and his cab disappear back down the driveway.

She took a deep, steadying breath. The stunning Italianate villa's plasterwork was bathed in an amber glow from the sunset.

Well...if Carlo says it's the right place, it must be.

She didn't know how Signor Chiesa had managed to find her a place this classy for her last night in Italy at no extra cost. It seemed pretty deserted. Perhaps they didn't have that many bookings?

She tightened her fingers on the handle of her briefcase and yawned, her frown lifting—and a weary smile forming. Why not enjoy it? After all, she'd earned a bit of extra luxury.

The last three weeks had been incredible. And utterly exhausting.

After several days in Venice negotiating with a family-run supplier who had been making luxury velvet since the seventeen hundreds, she'd headed to Tuscany and Puglia to source the most incredible wool and cotton blends. And for the last two weeks, she'd travelled throughout Lombardy, finishing at the silk weavers today—where she had commissioned some unique embroidered silks at a very reasonable price.

Of course, in the back of her mind the whole time had been the social media storm she'd caused in the US. Italy was far enough removed from the whole debacle she hadn't been dragged into it. But in a weird way, that had actually made her start to feel a little guilty—once her knee-jerk fury with Cade and his stupid bet had faded.

He'd been a total jerk. But she had been a bit of one, too.

She'd deleted the photos last week, but the damage had already been done. Not correcting the journalists she'd spoken to before leaving London about the state of their relationship, or rather non-relationship—just to annoy him—had also been a tad immature. She'd seen a huge increase in traffic to her website, so she didn't feel *that* bad. But now her buying trip was over, she would need to extricate herself from their fake relationship.

She walked up the steps into an enormous marble entrance hall—which was also surprisingly quiet. Where *were* the other guests? Was the place even open?

Who cares, frankly?

Tonight she needed a warm bath and then a long night's sleep in the lap of luxury.

Her energy levels had been on zero for days—a low-grade nausea making it hard for her to focus. And even though she'd loved the little *agriturismo* farm she'd used as her base in Lombardy, it would be quite nice not to have to make small talk in Italian over dinner with Signor Chiesa and his wife.

She rang the silver-plated bell on the mahogany reception desk nestled next to a lavish sweeping staircase. A young, smartly dressed woman appeared, wearing a tag which said *Alessia, Reception*, accompanied by a bellboy in full livery.

Wow, this place is seriously plush.

Charley struggled to control her grin. She was going to

have to send Signor Chiesa a thank-you message for arranging this.

'Signora Courtney, Aldo will take your items to your room,' the efficient young woman said in perfect English as the bellboy bowed and took Charley's briefcase, then disappeared. 'We have already put the rest of your luggage in the Como Suite.'

She had a whole suite in this beautiful place? Seriously? Charley felt the weariness ease a little more.

But before she could thank the manager, the woman was already leading her through a huge—and completely deserted—dining salon.

'Let me show you to the lakeside *terrazza*,' she announced. 'Where we have your evening meal waiting.'

'But I didn't order anything,' Charley said hastily, a little less pleased as she calculated the cost of a meal in a place like this.

The woman glanced over her shoulder and smiled. 'The meal is included in your accommodation, Signora Courtney.' And, because she was clearly a mind-reader, added, 'There is no extra to pay.'

'Oh, okay, *grazie*,' she said, not wanting to seem ungrateful—even though she wasn't sure she wanted a meal. She'd been queasy all day and had hardly eaten. But maybe the lack of food was precisely why she felt so depleted? And the menu here was bound to be amazing. Perhaps it would tempt her appetite out of hiding?

Charley followed the woman past the empty dining tables. They walked through a pair of elegantly appointed glass doors. The view was even more breathtaking on the wide terrace which wrapped around the building, the red-and-orange glow of the sunset casting a redolent light over

Lake Como and the centuries-old poplar trees, the water lapping gently against a private dock.

Charley sighed. The relaxed, perfectly appointed elegance of La Bella Grande was straight out of a luxury tourist brochure. The super-efficient receptionist led her to a single table, draped in white linen and laid with fine china and crystal stemware...for two people.

Charley frowned again as Alessia excused herself.

How odd. Was another one of the hotel's guests going to join her?

Her exhausted brain was still trying to process the table setting when she heard footsteps. A tall figure appeared, silhouetted in the dying sunshine, at the far end of the terrace and strode towards her. She blinked.

Was she hallucinating? Because he moved just like...

Then the light from the dining room illuminated dramatic features—and a deep husky voice sent shock waves through her fatigued body.

'Hello, Charlotte. About damn time you showed up.'

CHAPTER EIGHT

CADE LANDRY? In Lake Como? What the...?

'What are you doing in Italy?' Charley finally managed to ask, her head starting to ache.

And why do you look so gorgeous? she thought, annoyed with her physical response to him. Still.

The catastrophic frown on his face gave her the answer before he replied.

'I'm here to see you,' he said. 'Didn't you hear we're the new It Couple everyone back home is talking about?' His tone was low and husky, reminding her too forcefully of their one night together, but there was carefully leashed fury beneath—and the ruthless bite of disapproval. 'I've been taking the heat for three weeks for those photos. Now I've finally found you, I set up this meeting in private so we can get a few things straight.'

He sounded angry—*really* angry. And while she could sort of sympathise on one level—perhaps it had been a bit cowardly to throw him to the wolves, then high-tail it to Italy—his self-righteous tone, and the judgemental frown, had her own anger at the hurt he'd caused returning full force. Not to mention that he'd just completely ruined her surprise luxury lakeside break.

He must have been the one to pay for all this. It had never

been a lucky coincidence, a heaven-sent reward for all her hard work over the past three weeks. It had simply been a billionaire's trick to trap her so he could tell her off again, like he had four years ago.

Well, this time she wasn't going to run off with her tail between her legs.

'I get it. So *you're* the injured party now, are you?' she hurled the accusation back at him. 'When you were the one who chose to sleep with me on a bet?'

His scarred eyebrow launched up his forehead. *'What?'*

'You heard me. The asinine bet you made with my brother and his friend. I know all about it. Adam told me. The only-dating-one-woman-for-the-summer thing. That's why you're here, isn't it? Because you're stuck with me now so you can win some stupid property deal. But tell me, when did you decide it wasn't going to be me? That you would just use me and then discard me? While we were having the best sex of my life or before that? While you were deliberately seducing me with your dance skills?'

And why did you decide it couldn't be me? That I wasn't good enough?

The pathetic question echoed in her head, but she cut it off.

He'd made her feel cherished, and then he'd trashed it all. And hurt her, when she'd convinced herself long ago she couldn't be hurt. It would be funny if it didn't make her feel so exposed. How could she have fallen into the age-old trap of mistaking great sex for actual emotional engagement?

'And as if that isn't bad enough,' she carried on, because he seemed to have been struck dumb by her offensive, 'you bribed Carlo and Signor Chiesa to do your bidding. Of all the sneaky…'

'Wait a damn minute,' he roared, cutting off her outrage in full swing. '*You* ran out on *me*, not the other way around. And the bet had nothing to do with why I asked you to dance. Or why I slept with you. I wanted you and you wanted me and we were so damn good together I haven't been able to forget you. And believe me, I've tried.'

She took some solace from his angry acknowledgement their lovemaking had been special for him, as well, but then he spoilt that, too.

'But you're damn straight we're stuck together now for the rest of the summer—because acquiring Helberg is important to me and my business. And I'll be damned if I'll apologise for paying off whoever I had to, to get you here. Do you think I want to be in Italy, hiring out a whole hotel, just so I can talk with you in private because you were too immature to answer a single one of my texts or calls before blocking me? *Newsflash*, I don't. Any more than I wanted to be asked intrusive questions about my sex life by every celebrity hack from here to California… Questions you encouraged by making out like we were a couple in all the interviews and free publicity you got off the back of those photos.'

'I never said we were dating!' she managed in her defence, but the trickle of guilt at his outrage was starting to play footsie with the nausea in her stomach.

'You didn't deny it, though, did you?' he snarled. 'So here we damn well are.'

His angry words were still echoing across the lake— her own fury starting to choke her—when a young waiter cleared his throat loudly, making them both aware of his presence.

'*Signor, signorina*, would you like your antipasti now?' the poor boy asked, the two loaded plates in his hands trembling.

The nausea bounced into Charley's throat at the scent of roasted garlic. 'No,' she said.

At the exact same time, Cade commanded, 'Serve us, then leave.'

The waiter did Cade's bidding and shot off.

'Sit down,' Cade said, the low-grade fury suggesting he was holding on to his temper by a thread.

'I'm not eating with you,' she replied.

'Sit. Down. Now,' he demanded through gritted teeth before grabbing one of the chairs and smacking it down on the terrace. 'Or so help me, I will pick you up and put your butt in that chair myself.'

She glared at him. 'Go on then, manhandle me. All that makes you is a bully who is bigger than I am. As well as a sneak.'

She was not scared of his temper. The last thing she needed was to have a tussle with him, because she would probably lose, but she also knew he wouldn't hurt her. So she was more than ready to take her chances. And fight dirty if she had to.

He glared right back at her, the muscles she remembered admiring straining under the white shirt he wore with suit trousers. He thrust his fingers through his hair, dragging the thick waves back from his face, his movements stiff with anger. The charged silence seemed to snap between them, their standoff creating a force field of righteous fury and bruised egos.

But then he swung away and shouted a profanity into the

night air. When he turned back, his features had relaxed a fraction. Enough for her to see the frustration in his face.

'Sit down, Charlotte,' he said again, but this time his tone was more resigned than furious. 'I won't touch you.'

It was enough of a climb-down to let her keep her pride.

Grudgingly she perched her bottom on the chair he'd pulled out. But once she was seated, she was grateful for the support, because her knees had begun to shake.

She'd never been afraid of confrontation. Had always been ready to speak her mind. But maybe she'd been a bit too ready.

He lifted an expensive bottle of wine out of the ice bucket next to the table.

'You want a drink?' he asked.

She shook her head. This answer, at least, was easy.

He poured himself a generous glass, then took a gulp. She had the sense, though, he wasn't really tasting it.

'I don't bully women,' he said as he placed the glass on the starched linen tablecloth. 'And I refuse to feel bad for doing what I had to do to get you here. But my temper got out of hand, and for that I apologise.'

'Fine.' She nodded. 'Then I guess I can apologise for posting those photos without asking you first.'

'Okay. Apology accepted.' It wasn't exactly a truce, but it was close enough. Until he added, 'But now we need to talk about the consequences.'

'What consequences?'

'Don't play dumb, Charlotte,' he said, the edge back. 'I'm not about to forfeit Helberg. So you're gonna have to accompany me to the States tomorrow morning. And date me, in public at least, until Labor Day.'

She stared. Not really believing he could actually be serious. Unfortunately, though, he looked deadly serious.

'But that's...'

Ridiculous? Extreme? An over-reach of epic proportions?

She was so astounded at the steely determination in his expression she was speechless, for one whole second. 'I refuse to do it. I don't want to date you, in public or in private. We don't even like each other.'

'We like each other well enough,' he said implacably, as if he hadn't just yelled a profanity across Lake Como for most of Lombardy to hear.

'I see. Do you shout like that at all your girlfriends, then?'

'Nope, but I've never dated a woman before who's as contrary as you are,' he announced. Strangely, although frustration still tightened his tone, she could also see approval in his expression.

That would be the same approval which had derailed her common sense once before. The answering pulse of awareness in her belly, right alongside the nausea, only disturbed her more.

What was wrong with her? Cade Landry was a domineering alpha jerk. He was only here because he needed her to win a stupid bet—and he'd used underhanded methods to put her at his mercy. How could she possibly still be attracted to him?

'It won't work,' she said. 'Apart from the fact I have more important things to do than being your stunt date for the summer—such as setting up my workshop in London and working on my new commissions,' she added forcefully, to make it clear her business was just as important as his. 'We'd end up killing each…'

'Would those be the new commissions I helped you secure at the Broussards' *fais*?' he cut in, slicing through her indignation and making guilt flare in her queasy stomach.

'I don't see how that's relevant…?' she managed, determined to believe it wasn't.

So *what* if he'd helped introduce her around at the party? He'd only done it because he wanted to get into her knickers. And the quality of her work spoke for itself.

'Uh-huh…' He placed his elbow on the table and leant forward, which made her uncomfortably aware of the way his tailored shirt stretched across his pecs. 'Well, how about this for relevance? If you don't accompany me and pose as my loving girlfriend for the next five weeks, until Labor Day, I'll sue you for invasion of privacy, and using my name and image without my permission to garner free publicity for your business.'

She stiffened, shocked by the steely threat, and the flicker of challenge in the sapphire blue eyes. Was he getting off on this?

'You wouldn't dare!' she snapped. He was bluffing. He had to be. 'And anyway, it would be completely counterproductive… If you sued me, it would torpedo your chances of winning that bet.'

'Try me,' he murmured. 'But fair warning, Charlotte. You don't want to underestimate how ruthless a guy who grew up in the child welfare system in St Martin Parish, Louisiana—being bumped from one place to another like a piece of trash—can be. Or how dirty I'm prepared to fight to get what I want.'

She tensed, shocked by the ruthless tone and the brittle cynicism in his eyes.

But then her heart wedged in her throat as she noticed the muscle ticking in his jaw, and the scar which cut through the day-old stubble on his chin—and she digested what he had revealed about his past without intending to.

She'd been vaguely aware of the stories about his background. That he had grown up in foster care and come from nothing to build the Landry empire. It was all part of the self-made man myth which he had helped to promote. But there had been a raw note in his voice when he talked about the boy who had felt like trash, which was very different from the man she had met in San Francisco and all those years ago in Las Vegas. The charismatic, arrogant, supremely confident man who hadn't appeared to have a single chink in his armour.

And the strangest thought occurred to her.

Had she hurt him? By running out on him that morning?

She tried to bury the sentimental thought. She couldn't drop down that rabbit hole again, of believing they had shared more than an intense physical connection. But she couldn't seem to stop herself. It occurred to her his presence here, his decision to fly to Italy and buy out a whole hotel just to trap her into having a private dinner with him, and his determination to make her date him—rather than just dating no one for the rest of the summer to keep to the one date rule—didn't make a lot of sense.

She cut off the wayward thought because it wasn't helping with her nausea, especially when he picked up his fork and began to eat the antipasti, apparently waiting for her to capitulate. He ate calmly and methodically as if he didn't have a care in the world—and hadn't just threatened her with legal action to bend her to his will.

Think on that, Charley, before you start getting choked up about his difficult childhood.

Whatever Cade Landry had been through as a boy, he certainly wasn't vulnerable any more.

'Even if I wanted to, I can't spend the next five weeks in the US,' she said, trying for pragmatic, because having a pissing contest with someone as ruthless as he was not likely to end well for her. 'I've signed contracts, so my clients could sue me, too, if I don't deliver. And I'm about to start hiring seamstresses to help with the work who will be based in London.'

To her surprise, the muscle in his jaw relaxed.

'I have an event I want you to attend with me in Manhattan tomorrow night. But after that, I'll be based on the West Coast. You can't stay in London if we're gonna make this fly, but I can have my people organise suitable workspace in San Francisco and have anything you need shipped out to the West Coast so you can relocate your business there for the summer. You can hire whoever you want for the duration. All expenses paid, including their salaries.'

The offer was surprisingly generous and, annoyingly, more than a little tempting.

Adam had released the fifty thousand pounds from her trust fund, but money was still going to be tight until she saw the turnover from her new commissions. The salaries for the two seamstresses were also a big expense, because she wanted to hire the best.

But she wasn't ready to surrender yet…especially as she wasn't sure where the little leap in her belly—which felt too much like exhilaration—was coming from.

But then another problem occurred to her.

'Wait a minute. Are you expecting me to move in with you?' she asked, appalled.

Having to act as his loving girlfriend in public would be tough enough, but she was still stupidly attracted to Cade—probably for the simple reason he was the only man who had ever given her an orgasm. While she did not plan to beat herself up too much about the arousal pulsing insistently between her thighs, as she watched him eat in the sunset, she also did not want to tempt fate any more than was absolutely necessary.

He lowered his fork, but the instant denial she had been hoping for didn't come. Instead, his lips curved in the sensual smile which always made her blood pressure rise.

'I don't have a problem with exploring our chemistry some more. It's just sex after all. A basic physical urge which we happen to be very good at. You said yourself it was the best sex of your life.'

'Right,' she muttered, the telltale blush—which only he had ever been able to trigger—firing into her cheeks.

Why on earth had she blurted *that* out? Talk about giving the man ammunition.

'I'm not going to deny, it was damn good for me too,' he continued, not helping to diminish the blush one bit. 'But it wouldn't be part of the deal, no. You can live wherever you want—and I'll fund all your living expenses, just as long as you're close enough that I can call on you to accompany me to any and all events I choose to attend, some of which may be at short notice.'

'Okay, well, thanks for clarifying that,' she murmured grumpily.

So basically, she would be totally at his beck and call then. *Terrific.*

He chuckled, which made her feel even more exposed, and transparent. And wary.

It's just sex.

That's what he'd said. And he was right. So why couldn't she stop her heart beating too fast at the prospect of fake dating him?

He tore off a chunk of bread and used it to wipe the olive oil off his plate. 'Eat your supper and think about it,' he said far too easily. 'We can figure out all the details tomorrow before we fly out.'

She tensed at the definitive statement.

'I haven't said I'll go with you yet,' she protested, even though she wasn't sure she had much of a choice.

No doubt he was more than ruthless enough to follow through on his threat to sue. And in some ways, she couldn't blame him. She *had* created a media storm, however unintentionally. And while she was still super aggrieved at the thought of that stupid bet, this negotiation had at least established one thing.

Theirs was not and had never been an emotional connection.

Plus, if she was being entirely practical, the chance to have him pay for everything for a whole five weeks would be great for her business. She could work on the commissions and get the revenue from them into the bank to invest with her fifty thousand pounds when she returned to the UK. And dating him would give her loads more free publicity, because she intended to wear her own designs at every event he suggested.

Perhaps there was a way to turn this disaster into a professional opportunity?

'I'm also not that hungry,' she admitted.

His eyes narrowed, studying her with an intensity she found unsettling. 'You look washed out, Charlotte. Are you unwell?'

It was the last thing she had expected him to say. But even so, the silly flicker of emotion at the gruff concern in his voice shocked her.

'I'm fine…' she said, although she didn't feel fine. Not only was she exhausted and still feeling sick, her emotions were all over the place—especially where Cade Landry was concerned. Which could not be good. 'It's just…it's been a long three weeks. And I'd like to go to bed now—in the very expensive luxury suite you paid for so sneakily,' she added, unable to miss the opportunity for a final dig. 'To consider your proposal.'

He nodded, not reacting to the jab. But when she stood up, he stood, too.

He walked around the table and snagged her hand before she could make the speedy exit she'd planned. Rough calluses rasped against her palm and had a predictable effect on the pulsing in her sex. But before she could find the energy to tug her hand free, he had lifted her fingers to his lips and brushed a kiss across her knuckles.

The gesture was chivalrous, and strangely compelling, but not nearly as compelling as his husky tone when he added, 'I intend to make this work, Charlotte, for both of us. Get some sleep.' His lips curved in that tempting smile she remembered far too well. 'And enjoy the suite, which you'll be glad to hear cost me a fortune. We leave at ten tomorrow morning. We can discuss everything you need and make all the necessary arrangements on the flight to the US.'

She could have said no and argued with him some

more—but the arrogant assumption that she had capitulated already was tempered by his concerned expression. And the warmth of his touch.

She hadn't signed the lease yet for her new workspace in Shoreditch. She'd have to juggle a lot of stuff, but she could set things in motion on the plane tomorrow with his help. And she definitely planned to take full advantage of his financial support while posing as his stunt girlfriend. Not to mention tonight's suite. Knowing his sneakiness had cost him a fortune would be some consolation at least.

She gave a weary sigh and nodded. 'Fine, I'll come to the US, but I want my own place.'

'Sure.' His sensual smile made the pulse in her belly pound harder, though, the challenging expression unmistakeable.

She dragged her hand free but had to bunch her fingers into a fist to neutralise the buzz on her knuckles which was now playing havoc with the pulse in her sex.

As she trudged up to her room, she wanted to be furious with him—and with herself—for being forced into this position… She thought of Adam and his stake in the bet. She didn't want to make her brother lose Montague's, the jewellery company owned by Helberg, but frankly he was on his own for entering into such an idiotic agreement with Cade and Zane in the first place. Plus, she'd never quite understood why buying back their mother's old jewellery company meant so much to him. Their mum had taken no interest in it herself at the time of her death, as far as Charley could remember.

As she sank into a hot bath in the enormous clawfoot tub in front of a marble terrace which looked out over the lake, it occurred to her she wasn't angry with Cade any

more, because all she really felt was hopelessly confused.
And even a little scared, thanks to the flicker of anticipation in her stomach alongside the nausea.

Because that flicker reminded her of the girl who
couldn't resist taking stupid risks simply to make herself
feel valued—which she had always ended up regretting.

What she needed to remember was that Cade Landry
was a dangerous man, because he had the power to make
her *want* to do those impulsive, reckless things again, no
matter what the consequences...

CHAPTER NINE

SOMETHING'S WRONG.

Cade frowned as Charlotte slept in the leather seat opposite him in the Landry jet.

Why did she still look so exhausted? And why did he feel uncomfortable about the fact she hadn't put up more of a fight this morning? Wasn't having her at his mercy exactly what he'd flown out to Lake Como to achieve?

But he couldn't shake the uneasiness in his gut as he observed the slow rise and fall of her breathing.

He'd been braced for an argument when she'd appeared for breakfast at the hotel. So he'd made sure he was well ahead of her—by setting up a team to relocate her business to San Francisco for the rest of the summer and getting his EA to handle any issues with her visa status. But there had been no fuss, no more angry words. Instead she'd spent breakfast discussing options for her workspace and accommodations with his property management team on the West Coast while picking at her food.

From the fascinating conversation he'd listened in to with interest, he'd discovered she was a smart, erudite businesswoman who knew what she wanted but could also be flexible and take expert advice when needed. Both qualities Cade considered invaluable when making a startup like hers a success.

She'd appeared worn-out last night, once he'd taken the time to really look at her. And while she'd finished what needed to be done this morning once they had boarded the Landry jet in Milan—settling on a space hire in the Embarcadero and a condo in the same building as his—she'd barely touched her lunch before dropping back to sleep.

He'd driven himself to exhaustion too, once—especially during the early days—pulling eighteen- and twenty-hour shifts, fuelled on coffee and adrenaline and ambition for weeks on end. He knew what it looked like when the inevitable crash came. So why was he so upset at the thought of Charlotte burning herself out?

Her welfare wasn't his concern.

But as she shifted on the seat—struggling to find a comfortable position—he undid his belt. Touching her probably wasn't smart. He'd learned that yesterday evening when her stunned reaction to his knuckle buzz had left him hard and aching. But he needed her well-rested by the time they hit New York. Being photographed at the party tonight would establish her as his summer date—and hopefully give the media what they wanted so they would leave him the hell alone. Plus, he hoped to run into Zane deMarco—who had some explaining to do about the candid shots of him getting up close and personal with a Helberg employee at a pretzel stand while he had already racked up at least one other date for the summer so far.

He unclipped Charlotte's belt and scooped her into his arms.

Her eyes opened just as he got a lungful of her scent.

The streak of sensation hitting his groin wasn't helped by the sight of her wide green eyes and her heavy sigh.

'What are you doing?' she murmured, still groggy.

'Taking you to the bedroom in back,' he said. 'I want you awake when we get to New York.'

She blinked, but instead of protesting, she looped an arm around his neck, tucked her head against his collarbone, and yawned. Her warm breath brushed his neck, sending the sensations in his gut into free fall.

'Thanks, Sir Galahad,' she mumbled.

After placing her on the bed, he eased off her sneakers and tucked the quilt over her, the arrow in his gut becoming sharp and insistent.

The constriction in his ribs tightened as she turned away from him and curled onto her side, fast asleep again.

Just sex. And chemistry.

He headed back to his seat, determined to work for the rest of the flight. But he couldn't shake the disturbing thought that his motives for chasing Charlotte all the way to Italy, and blackmailing her into returning to the US with him, might be about more than just the bet he had to win...

'How are you feeling, Charlotte?'

Charley forced a strained smile at the low question from the man sitting opposite her in the chauffeur-driven car— who looked typically devastating in a designer suit—as they cut through the snarl of evening traffic in Manhattan's Meatpacking District.

'Fabulous. Bring it on,' she said, trying to sound confident and bold, despite the knots in her stomach.

At least the low-grade nausea of the last few days had faded after her catatonic-like sleep on his plane. She'd had a solid six hours to add to the ten hours in Italy the night before. She still didn't feel entirely herself, but she felt better than she had when she'd agreed to this charade—give or take the odd heart bump and the hot pulse in her abdomen every time she was near her fake date.

Although this arrangement didn't feel particularly fake any more.

Especially after she had woken up on the plane to find him carrying her to bed with that watchful expression on his face.

He had been staring at her the same way ever since his car had picked her up at the stylist's ten minutes ago—as if he were assessing her well-being.

'We don't have to stay long. I've booked you a suite at the hotel the event is at for tonight,' he added. 'Then we fly to the West Coast tomorrow.'

'Thanks,' she managed.

She hadn't seen him since they'd landed at JFK four hours ago. After disembarking, she'd been whisked off to a private beauty therapist's—where she had been primped to within an inch of her life—and then the stylist's, where a selection of her designs had been waiting for her.

'And thanks for getting my wardrobe shipped over in time for tonight,' she added.

'It was part of our deal,' he said simply.

True, so why did it feel like more?

Cade Landry was a take-charge, demanding guy who got things done—and his competence was as sexy as the way he filled out a tuxedo. But why did this situation suddenly feel so overwhelming?

He'd thought of everything in preparation to present

her as his date at this event—and establish their status as a couple.

It's about the bet, Charley. Remember that.

She smoothed her palms down her gown. The sky-blue tulle and chiffon creation was a prototype she had been working on for months. The exposure it would get Trouble Maker at a statement party like this one was going to be invaluable.

Surely that was why she was nervous? After all, she had once revelled in showing off for the media—back in her bad old days. The nerves couldn't have anything to do with the scent of his woodsy, spicy cologne, which brought back a host of other disturbing memories.

The car pulled to the kerb in front of a huge brutalist building which towered over this entrance to the High Line, the camera flashes visible through the tinted windows.

He stepped out of the car and leaned back in—blocking her from the chaos outside—to offer her his arm.

'Let's do this, Charlotte,' he murmured, the low Southern accent rippling over her skin as his eyes deepened with encouragement, and that disturbing approval.

Her unruly heartbeat and the knots in her stomach went haywire.

'Sure thing, Sir Galahad,' she quipped back, trying to even her breathing as she climbed out. He shielded her from the cameras, and the shouts of the photographers and celebrity journalists. But as the muscles in his forearm tensed beneath her fingers, her sex clenched in unison.

When was she going to stop feeling so attuned to this man?

They ran the gauntlet together with his arm around her the whole way. As if she were special to him, when she knew she wasn't. They were ushered into one of the private lifts, alone.

She let out a relieved breath. 'Well, that was hideous.'

'It should keep them happy for a while,' he murmured, still watching her with eagle-sharp eyes.

'I'm just hoping they got a good shot of my dress, and they remember to mention Trouble Maker,' she managed.

How did he do that? Suck all the oxygen out of the lift? Because he'd done the exact same thing four years ago in that lobby in Vegas… And why would she rather suffocate than step away from him?

A smile curved his lips, as if he knew the war she was waging with herself.

Good grief, was she still so transparent?

'I'll have my press people make sure they mention the dress,' he said. His gaze travelled over her figure, sparking a predictable endorphin rush. 'It's striking,' he murmured. 'But not as striking as the woman wearing it.'

'Are you trying to flatter me into submission now?' she asked, aiming for flippant, but getting breathless instead.

'Is it working?'

'It doesn't need to,' she said as the air continued to clog in her lungs. 'You've already got me exactly where you want me.'

'Not quite.' He touched her cheek with his thumb, then skimmed it down the side of her face.

She shivered instinctively, the naked need in his eyes shocking her. But still, she couldn't step away from the flame.

'I want you back in my bed, Charlotte.' He trailed his thumb across her lips, and they trembled. 'And I think you want to be there, too.'

His hand settled on her neck, that dangerous thumb stroking the giddy pulse in her collarbone.

She should tell him to take a hike. It's what they'd agreed to. But how could she? When they both knew he was right. And she'd never been a good liar.

The lift bell pinged, and a breath gushed out of her lungs.

Saved by the bell, literally.

The doors opened onto a lavish lobby area, accented in vintage mahogany and butter-soft leather. The staggering view across the Hudson River to Jersey City looked impossibly enchanting despite the throb of sound and fury coming from the DJ manning the decks in the party space beyond. The view, though, was nowhere near as heart-stopping as the glint of purpose in his eyes.

Could he see her need? Feel the pulsing ache which had been driving her nuts since he'd appeared in Lake Como?

Probably!

'Showtime,' he murmured.

But as he took her arm and led her into the party, it wasn't the strobe lighting, or the wall of noise, or the press of bodies making her heart pound.

It was the giddy pulse of arousal—and something more—every time he introduced her as his, every time his palm settled possessively on her back or her hip or her waist, every time he leaned close to shout something witty or provocative above the throbbing beat of the music—and everything his words kept echoing in her head, a tantalising promise, impossible to deny.

I want you back in my bed, Charlotte. And I think you want to be there, too.

I'm out of the bet. I don't want it. You and Adam carry on without me.

Zane deMarco was out of the running for Helberg.

Cade knew he should feel elated as he watched the guy

disappear after the pretty brunette from Helberg's HQ—
who was not the date who had arrived at the event on de-
Marco's arm. This development was better than anything
Cade had hoped for when he'd cornered Zane on the bal-
cony outside while Charlotte was in the restroom. But the
stunned look on Zane's face when the Helberg woman had
stormed through the crowd towards him, looking ready
to murder the corporate raider, had soured the moment
somehow.

What was going on between deMarco and the Helberg
chick? And why did Cade feel unsettled about the way
whatever it was had made Zane throw in the towel so easily?

Stepping back into the party, he spotted Charlotte
coming out of the restroom. Something deep and visceral
tugged hard in his gut. And he headed through the crowd of
dancers towards her, determined to forget about the damn
bet for the rest of the night.

She'd done her part this evening without an argument.
Acted like they were a couple for the cameras and then
danced with him—her slender body gyrating in his arms,
effortlessly seductive, while also being frustratingly just
out of reach.

Everything was working out just how he wanted it. So
why did he feel so on edge?

Her gaze locked with his as he reached her, and he saw
something fierce and yet guarded in her eyes. Something
which sharpened the arrow of need in his gut. And suddenly he knew why.

He'd been by her side all evening, inhaling her intoxicating scent and feeling her shiver of response every time
he touched her—those casual, intimate touches between

couples that were supposed to be for show, but hadn't been, ever since he had cornered her in the elevator.

He grasped her hand. 'We're done here.'

Her eyebrows shot up. 'Excuse me?' she said, as if she didn't know exactly where tonight had always been heading.

'We're leaving,' he added, tugging her through the crowd.

The elevator in the entrance area had too many people to catch it, so he slammed his palm against the emergency exit and took the stairwell.

'Cade, what on earth...' she cried, her fingers tugging against his hold as he took the stairs to the penthouse level. 'Where are you taking me?'

'To your suite,' he said and tightened his grip.

His EA had given him a key card for her room, which he was supposed to pass to her once they were through at the event. That had been the plan, anyway, to escort her to the suite, then head to his place on Fifth and meet her at the airport tomorrow for their flight to San Francisco.

To hell with that.

They needed to establish some ground rules for the next month, or this arrangement was going to be unworkable. And ground rule number one was to stop pretending this was just about the bet. Because it was also about the sex.

The memory of her in his bed was still giving him hell—pheromones-wise—but worse was the memory of the morning after, when he'd woken up to find her note.

That he was still hung up about that note made it clear they had unfinished business. Business they could only finish by dealing with the sexual tension which had been building between them all night.

He pressed the key card against the door to the High
Line Suite and marched inside. The darkness through the
room's glass walls glittered with the lights from the Jersey
shore and the boats on the Hudson. The spectacular view
didn't register, though, as he swung around to press Charlotte against the wall and cup her flushed cheeks.

'Tell me you don't want this, too,' he demanded, 'and
I'll back off.' But he'd be damned if he was going to avoid
stating the obvious any longer.

She stared at him, her lips pursing into a tight line, but
her beautiful eyes had dilated almost to black.

'I suppose you think the caveman approach is a turn-
on,' she said, but beneath the sharp tone was the husky
note he recognised.

'Are you telling me it isn't?' he challenged her, brushing
the ridge of his growing erection against her belly.

She didn't push him away. Their showdown bristled
with energy, but unlike the one in Lake Como, this time
it was heady desire, not anger, which sizzled and sparked
between them.

He kissed her neck, captured the pulse thundering in
her collarbone, and began to feast on the sweet, sultry taste
of her skin.

She swore, then let out a shuddering sigh. And grasped
his head to draw him closer.

The last of his control snapped like a high-tension wire,
his hands cupping her butt, finding firm, naked flesh beneath the dress.

Another thong, bless the Lord.

She relaxed into the kiss, lifting her leg to hook it around
his hip, notching the erection in his pants against the tender spot between her thighs.

He rubbed her through their clothing, feeling the ripples of her response, revelling in the delicious musk of her arousal.

She gasped, her head thudding back against the wall, undulating her hips to locate the perfect contact, to demand more.

'We need to be naked...' she managed.

He lifted his head, his mind fraying, her bold request reflected in the shocked arousal in her gaze—which was as vivid and desperate as his own.

'Yeah,' he guttered out. But as he fumbled to find her zipper, frantic to feast on her again, she shifted back and batted his urgent hands away.

'Let me. I don't want you to rip it.'

He laughed, the indignation on her face releasing some of the tension in his gut.

But as she stripped off the floaty blue fabric and wriggled it past her hips, leaving her in nothing but her bra and thong, the tension cinched tight again.

He cradled one breast, brushed his thumb across the rouged tip visible through the lace.

Damn, had her breasts got fuller, or was that his overactive imagination? Because she looked magnificent. She'd always been beautiful, but her figure seemed lusher and even more mouth-watering than it had their first night.

She jolted against him, the soft sob enough to turbocharge his own arousal.

He lifted her breast from its lacy prison and captured the stiff peak in his mouth. He suckled hard as her nipple hardened against his tongue. She thrust her fingers into his hair, her body shuddering violently, her response nothing short of electric.

'That's so good...' she cried.

He delved beneath the satin thong with urgent fingers to find her hot and wet and ready.

She bucked as he worked the swollen nub, his lips still devouring her breast.

He thrust one finger into the tight sheaf, but seconds later, she sobbed as her orgasm pulsed around him.

As she came down, he drew back and licked her dew off his fingers. The throbbing need in his groin was unbearable. She looked spent, dishevelled, her bra half off, her panties soaked with her release. He could smell her, that sultry, flowery scent, as her eyes opened. She looked dazed. Her climax so much faster than before.

'Again?' he asked, his need so strong now he wasn't sure he could stay sane much longer.

She nodded.

He fumbled to find the condom in his wallet, shrugged off his jacket, then ripped open the fly of his suit pants.

She stared at the thick erection, watching him with heavy-lidded eyes as he rolled on the protection with clumsy fingers.

'Turn around, Charlotte,' he demanded.

For once she didn't argue, bracing her hands on the wall, presenting him with the flushed flesh of her butt. The pain in his groin became immense. He needed to be inside her now.

He captured her breasts from behind, holding her steady as he plunged deep. Her swollen flesh was exquisitely tight, but so slick he lodged himself to the hilt in one powerful thrust. He dropped one hand to find her clitoris and pressed his thumb against it, desperate to make her shatter again before he did.

He established a punishing rhythm. The slap of flesh against flesh echoed around the quiet room alongside her sobs and his grunts. The pleasure built at the base of his spine, the pressure becoming exquisite pain, as he slammed into her and she pressed back to take more of him...to take it all.

He shouted as her sex clenched, her climax triggering his own brutal orgasm. The pleasure crested at last, the orgasm exploding through his nerve endings as everything he was, everything he wanted, became a blur of brutal need. And desperate release.

Charley pressed her forehead against the wall, with Cade's big body holding her up while also leaning heavily against her back.

His hand twitched, still cupping her breast. She flinched, aware of how sensitive her breasts had been, and how quickly she had shot to orgasm. Twice.

'You, okay?' he murmured into her hair, his voice as rough as she felt.

'I think so...' she said, not entirely sure.

When had she ever felt so raw? And so sated?

She hadn't intended to have sex with him again, but when he'd grasped her hand twenty minutes ago, the purpose in his gaze like a brand on her too-sensitive skin, and marched her down to the suite—after several hours of dancing—she hadn't been able to resist. Or object. Because she'd wanted him with the same urgency.

He shifted behind her, then drew out of her body.

Her tight flesh released the huge erection with difficulty, making her flinch again.

He grasped her hips, turning her to face him. She folded

her arms over her chest and the remnants of her underwear, feeling exposed as he adjusted his own clothing.

She couldn't stop shivering. The sex, the need, had been so basic, so elemental, she hadn't given a single thought to the repercussions of what she was doing. Or the fact that the tourists on the evening cruises below could have watched everything.

'Hey?' he said, cradling her cheek, already fully clothed again, unlike her. 'You sure you're okay? That was kind of intense.'

She nodded, then forced a smile. 'I certainly hope no one on those boats has binoculars, or we just gave them quite a show.'

He let out a rough chuckle. 'I certainly hope the glass is treated, or I'm gonna sue!'

But as their laughter died, the awkwardness returned. She should ask him to leave, to create some space and distance between them. But she couldn't shift the knot in her throat, or the wave of emotion which suddenly threatened to level the last of her common sense.

She looked away from those piercing blue eyes which seemed to see so much more than she wanted them to. 'I need to take a shower.'

'Want me to join you?' he asked.

She laughed. The man was nothing if not persistent.

'Given what just happened, I'm not sure that's a good idea,' she said, but as she went to walk away, desperate to maintain what was left of her dignity—her mind racing with all the implications of what they'd just done—he snagged her wrist.

'I hope you know, Charlotte. There's no way of putting

this genie back in its bottle. And I sure as hell don't want to, do you?'

She should tell him she did, because that was the safest course. She had committed to spending five weeks on his arm. Sleeping with him would only confuse things more. But the knot in her throat swelled, cutting off the denial, and forcing her to blurt out the truth.

'I honestly don't know,' she managed.

He tipped his head to one side, studying her for what felt like an eternity. Then he dropped his forehead to hers, his hands resting on her bare hips, making her more aware of her nakedness. 'How about we both take a shower—'

'I don't think...'

'Separately,' he interrupted her interruption before the panic could take hold. 'This place has two bathrooms,' he added, ever practical. 'But then I'd like to stay the night.'

The possessive demand made her heartbeat jump in her chest, Still she couldn't find the will to tell him no. To establish any boundaries. And not just because she felt washed out, both emotionally and physically. But also because she wanted to be held, the way he had held her once before. She'd run out on him then. And maybe that was why this need had come back to bite them both on the arse.

Perhaps it really was just a case of getting this desire— and the yearning for his approval, which had to be a hold-over from her childhood—out of her system once and for all.

She nodded. 'Okay.'

She spent a good twenty minutes scrubbing the scent of him off her over-sensitised body in the shower. But after pulling on an old T-shirt, she found him lying in the huge double bed, waiting for her. With his dark hair damp and slicked back from that extraordinary face, and his chest bare—the phoenix tattoo flaring over one broad shoulder—her heart thundered against her ribs again.

Why did he have to look so irresistible? It wasn't fair.

He lifted the sheet, beckoned her into the bed. 'Don't panic, Charlotte. I don't plan to ravish you again…tonight. I just want to make sure you're okay.'

She was pretty sure letting him care for her would only make things more dangerous. But she felt too tired to argue, or deny the pulse of longing, the swell of emotion making the knot in her throat start to ache.

Where was the harm in letting him watch over her for one night? When she felt so raw and on edge… She could establish that all-important distance after she'd regained her strength, and her sense of purpose, tomorrow.

No man had ever claimed her so comprehensively. Maybe she should give herself a break for feeling needy right now.

She climbed into the bed, rested her head on his shoulder as he tucked her against his side, and let the steady thuds of his heartbeat under her ear lull her into deep, dreamless sleep.

CHAPTER TEN

WHEN CHARLEY WOKE the next morning, groggy and sore, it took her a moment to figure out where she was as the stream of sunlight illuminated the room's luxurious furniture and stunning view. Then she became aware of Cade's arm wrapped around her waist.

She could feel his breath, slow and steady on her nape, feel his warmth against her back, cocooning her. But the moment of calm, the feeling of security, was quickly obliterated by the twist of nausea in her belly.

She flung back the sheet as the twist sharpened and threatened to surge.

She raced across the thick carpeting, vaguely aware of Cade's voice—husky with sleep—asking what was wrong behind her. She reached the bathroom just in time to flip up the toilet seat and heave.

Her tender stomach felt as if it were turning inside out as she lost everything she had eaten the night before. She didn't hear him come into the bathroom until his hand stroked her hair back from her face.

Finally the endless retching stopped, and she collapsed onto the bathroom's marble tiles, shaking.

She was vaguely aware of the sound of running water. He handed her a dampened flannel.

'All through?' he asked, his voice grave.

She nodded despite the achy exhaustion and the still jumpy sensation in her belly as she wiped her face. 'It must have been something I ate,' she said weakly.

This should be excruciatingly embarrassing, but she felt too awful to care.

He handed her a toothbrush. As soon as the peppermint scent of the paste he'd added hit her senses, her stomach rebelled again.

She grasped the bowl, leaning over with a moan to retch some more. But mercifully there was nothing left to come up.

She felt fragile and pathetically grateful for his presence as he helped her off the floor and guided her back to the bed when she had finally finished vomiting.

'I'm calling a doctor,' he said, his phone in his hand.

'Don't be silly. It's just a stomach bug.'

He ignored her, but she felt too rubbish to argue further as she listened to him contacting one of his assistants and ordering them to have the nearest medic sent to the suite.

Embarrassment scorched her cheeks when he finished the call.

'Get some rest,' he said. 'The doctor will be here soon.'

She lifted her aching head and turned over to stare at him. He sat in the chair opposite, having donned his shirt as well as his trousers.

'This is silly,' she said. 'I'm sure I'll be fine now. I've been needing to do that for days.'

His forehead furrowed. 'What do you mean? For days?'

'I've been a bit queasy for a while, that's all. And tired. It must be a bug that's going round.'

'So not something you ate?' he said, his eyes narrowing.

'Well, no, maybe not.'

'Exactly how long have you been feeling nauseous?' Why did he sound so annoyed?

Her tired mind tried to grasp his mood, but she couldn't seem to grasp much of anything at all. 'Only a week or so.'

'A *week*?' He cursed. 'Why didn't you tell me before I dragged you to the party last night?' he added, confusing her more. It was impossible to tell from his expression whether he was angry with her now, or himself.

'Would it have made a difference?' she asked.

'Of course. I'm not a monster, Charlotte,' he said, getting increasingly aggrieved by the second, which only fascinated her more. 'I wouldn't have made you spend all evening on your feet. And I sure as hell would never have touched you if I'd known you were sick. You should have told me.'

'I didn't feel sick last night though. I think that was fairly obvious.'

He paced across the room, looking more agitated than she had ever seen him.

This was new. But while her stomach still felt super-delicate—and the heat in her cheeks at the thought of vomiting in front of him wasn't exactly abating either—his agitation was somehow reassuring.

In fact, she almost enjoyed it when the knock sounded on the door and he shot across the room to answer it.

Who knew? The way to make Cade Landry lose his cool, and that cast-iron control, was to puke your guts up in front of him.

He stood beside the bed, tapping his bare foot on the carpet, hovering over her as the nice Dr Ramirez introduced himself, then started to ask a lot of questions.

The doctor took her blood pressure, checked her pupils, then asked her more questions. But as Cade got more agitated, she found herself relaxing. The nausea had finally faded. And it was almost sweet to have Cade so concerned. About her.

When she was a child, she'd always felt like a burden whenever she was sick. She knew the staff had been paid to look after her because her mother was too fragile to spend any time with her and her father was always working—or banging his latest bit on the side—and her older brother was away at boarding school.

How strange to have that yearning for someone care to enough about her to look the way Cade looked now—agitated and worried—finally fulfilled in these circumstances.

But then her own composure took a major hit.

'Is there any chance you could be pregnant, Ms Courtney?' the doctor asked.

'No... What? *No!*' she sputtered, refusing to look at Cade.

'I see. When did you have your last period?'

Her mind slammed into a wall of sheer panic as she tried to remember the date. She hadn't had one in a while. But her menstrual cycle had always been erratic. 'I... I'm not sure. I'd have to check my phone.'

She was forced to look at Cade when he scooped up her purse and handed it to her. To her astonishment, his agitation had disappeared. But then, she couldn't gauge his reaction to the doctor's line of questioning because his expression had gone completely blank.

It took her forever to locate her phone, switch it on and open her calendar app. But as she scrolled through the weeks—looking for the red *P* she always stuck into the app to keep track of her cycle—panic started to claw at her throat.

By the time she finally located the *P*, then counted the weeks in between, her fingers were trembling. She lifted her head.

The doctor had a kindly, encouraging smile on his face. Cade, though, who stood behind him, was staring at her with an intensity she recognised, his stance rigid.

She wasn't pregnant. That would be nuts. He'd worn a condom that night. And they'd only done it the once.

'Charlotte, how long?' Cade prompted, his voice controlled, but with an edge which suggested he was holding on to his composure by his fingertips.

'Um…well, it's been a little over seven weeks… But really that's not unusual. I have a very irregular cycle,' she rushed to clarify, her cheeks burning now, because talking about her menstrual cycle with this man felt more intimate than having him inside her.

Which was almost as ludicrous as the notion she might be carrying his child.

This isn't happening. It can't be. It's too absurd.

But even as she tried desperately to convince herself the doctor had to be mistaken, all the ways in which her body had changed—the things she had dismissed as the emotional and physical stress of kick-starting her business and the fallout from her night with Cade in San Francisco—suddenly coalesced in her head into a burning pile of incontrovertible proof.

Her sore, heavy, oversensitive breasts. The queasiness which had begun over a week ago. The fact she'd had her last period three weeks before she'd slept with Cade that first night. Yes, her cycle was erratic, but not *that* erratic.

She pressed her hand to her stomach.

'And did you have sexual relations during that time?' the doctor asked gently, oblivious to Charley's shock and that strange feeling of horrified awe which was now pressing down on her chest.

Charley's gaze met Cade's. 'Um…yes, once,' she murmured. 'About four and a half weeks ago. But we used protection.'

'What kind of protection?' the doctor asked.

'A condom.' Cade's deep voice cut through the feeling of unreality. 'Which I was too distracted to check afterwards.'

The doctor nodded—still so calm, as if Charley's life wasn't going into free fall.

'Condoms are usually very reliable, Mr Landry.' He turned to address Cade. 'But I would still advise a pregnancy test. The symptoms Ms Courtney has described to me are very common in the first trimester.'

'How do we do that?' Cade asked, taking charge, because Charley had totally lost the power of speech now—her emotions pitching on a stormy sea of questions without answers.

Could I have made a baby? With Cade Landry? What if I have a life? Growing inside me? How do I even feel about that?

'You can get an over-the-counter test—they're very accurate—or I could arrange a blood test this morning at my office on West Twenty-Fifth Street…'

'We'll take the blood test,' Cade said with his usual pragmatism.

Charley should have been annoyed—this was her body he was talking about—but she couldn't seem to feel much of anything at the moment.

As the next hour passed, she sank deeper into the fog.

Cade accompanied her to the private medical facility in Chelsea. She had to sign a ton of forms, the nurse drew a vial of blood, and five minutes later they were led into Dr Ramirez's office. The clean white space looked out over the Hudson River, the scent of expensive leather and potpourri doing nothing to cover the scent of the man beside her.

She could have objected to Cade being there, but it seemed pointless.

The realisation they would always share this moment made her pulse race when Dr Ramirez appeared. And cut straight to the chase.

'Your blood test is conclusive, Ms Courtney. Given the date of your last menstruation, that would make you just over seven weeks pregnant.'

With Cade Landry's child.

The blood rushed out of her head to pound in her heart. Cade asked a string of pragmatic, surprisingly measured questions. But she couldn't hear them…because all she could hear were the clear, unequivocal thoughts in her head. Thoughts she never would have expected in these circumstances, but were there nonetheless.

How this happened, why it happened—or how impossible this situation is—doesn't matter. All I know is that this is my child. As well as Cade's. And I want to have it.

But how did that even work? When she had never considered becoming a mother until this precise moment…and had no confidence whatsoever she would be a good one?

Cade sat across from Charlotte in the limo as they headed out of the Midtown tunnel en route to JFK.

He'd made an executive decision to fly straight to San

Francisco—and told his assistant to arrange to have Charlotte's luggage collected from the hotel on the High Line.
They needed time to regroup and take stock without having to deal with any press attention.

Charlotte hadn't objected. But then, she hadn't said much
of anything at all.

She was staring out the window of the car now, but he
doubted she was seeing the buildings of downtown Brook-
lyn. She looked shell-shocked. He knew the feeling.

A baby. A child. *His* child.

He had no idea how to process the news they'd just
been dealt by the doctor. And he had no doubt at all she
was struggling to process it too, given that her hands were
clasped so tightly in her lap the knuckles had whitened.

It felt as if they had entered an alternative reality. And
there was no way to get back to normality ever again. The
one thing he could process, though, was a fierce sense of
protectiveness—towards both Charlotte and the child.

Weird on one level. Because he had never thought of becoming a father. But not that weird on another. Hadn't he
spent his whole life building a legacy he could be proud of?
Why had it never occurred to him until now that it would
mean nothing if he had no one to pass his business on to?

But as he watched Charlotte—trying to gauge her reaction—he knew this wasn't a child yet. It wasn't even a baby.
It was simply a pregnancy. And for him to feel so protective already—to be envisioning Charlotte's slender body
heavy with his baby—was premature. What if she didn't
wish to keep his child?

He cleared his throat. Her head jerked round and her
gaze met his, her expression that of someone who had been
woken from a trance.

'How does your stomach feel?' he asked. The doctor had given him a ton of advice about the morning sickness because he'd quizzed the guy while Charlotte had sat beside him in silence.

She placed a hand on her stomach, her throat contracting as she swallowed. 'Okay, I guess.'

It bothered him that he couldn't gauge her reaction, because all he could see was shock.

One of his greatest assets in business was his ability to read people and act accordingly to get what he wanted. Not being able to figure out how she felt about the pregnancy was a problem, forcing him to break cover.

'How do *you* feel? About having this baby?'

She stared. Her bottom lip started to tremble. She bit into it.

'I want to have it,' she said at last. The relief he felt was palpable. Then she added, 'But I'm also absolutely terrified.'

He could see her fear was genuine, and wondered where it came from. But before he could ask her about it, she said, 'And you? How do *you* feel?'

'Shocked,' he admitted. 'But also kind of thrilled.'

Her eyes widened, her pale skin flushing. Clearly she hadn't expected that answer.

'Really? You *want* to become a dad?' she said, sounding incredulous. 'I thought you'd try and pressure me into having a termination.'

He should have been insulted…but he let the knee-jerk reaction go. Because she was right about one thing. He hadn't actually thought of becoming a *dad*, per se.

The baby, *his* baby, represented a legacy to him first and foremost—a part of himself which was even now growing inside her womb. Strictly speaking it wasn't the thought of becoming a father, but rather that fierce sense of possession and vindication—at the thought of Charlotte not only having his child but also nurturing it, the way his mother had never nurtured him—which thrilled him.

But before he started examining his own reaction, he wanted to examine hers. Their current situation wasn't ideal. If they were going to negotiate this bombshell, they would need to work together. So it might be good to find out, when she had decided he was a total jerk?

'Why would you think I'd do something like that?' he asked.

'Because...' She huffed. 'Well, you're *you.*'

He coughed out a laugh, not sure whether to be insulted now or amused.

'Are you trying to say you think I'm a selfish bastard without *saying* I'm a selfish bastard?'

It was supposed to be a joke, but when she studied him, he wasn't sure he wanted to hear her answer.

'I don't know you well enough to know if you're a complete bastard,' she said. 'But I do think you're deeply cynical. And arrogant. And that you make sure you always get what you want—no matter the collateral damage. Which reminds me, rather unfortunately, of my father...' Before he could ask her about the man, she carried on. 'Then again, you held my hair while I was puking this morning—and took care of me when I didn't expect you to, which makes you not quite as much of a bastard as he was.'

'Gee, thanks,' he said, well and truly damned by her faint praise. What had she expected? That he would ignore her, or worse, be squeamish about a little vomit? 'Your old man sounds like a real peach,' he added.

'You have no idea,' she said. 'How about yours? Did you know him?'

'Nope,' he said, then added, before he could think better of it, 'I doubt my mother knew who he was either.'

'I'm sorry to hear that,' she said, sympathy shadowing her eyes.

'Why?' he asked, determined to deflect her pity. 'It doesn't sound like you got much out of knowing your old man.'

'True,' she said. 'But I'm not sure it's a good thing that neither of us has first-hand knowledge of what a dad is supposed to do.'

'I guess not,' he said, glad the flicker of pity had disappeared.

'I appreciate your directness about the pregnancy,' she continued, but the sadness and confusion still lurked in her eyes. 'I've got to admit, you're not the sort of man I would *ever* have expected to be thrilled about an accidental pregnancy. Especially with a woman like me.'

'Exactly what kind of woman do you think you are?' he asked, wanting to make this about her again instead of him.

'It's not what kind of woman *I* think I am. It's what kind of woman *you* think I am.'

'Uh-huh. Enlighten me,' he said, both annoyed and oddly intrigued by her candour.

'Reckless, impulsive, immature, entitled,' she said, her tone flat and pragmatic. But he could see the hurt in her eyes, hear the defensiveness—and the echo of the fragile girl he'd first met. 'Basically, not the kind of woman you'd want to be the mother of your child,' she continued. 'If you'd had a choice.'

'You're right, you are reckless and impulsive,' he said, because he'd be damned if he'd sugar-coat his opinion of her. After all, she certainly hadn't sugar-coated her opinion of him. 'But entitled and immature?' he continued, determined to prove that while he might be arrogant and cynical, he wasn't as dumb as she thought he was. 'I may have seen that when we first met. I don't see it any more.'

'Perhaps you better tell me what you *do* see now...' she said, but then she turned away to stare back out the car window. And he realised she was braced to hear the worst—which made him consider his words carefully. He wanted to be honest, but he also had no desire to hurt that girl again.

'I think you're passionate, smart, brutally honest and hard-working, and someone who is not afraid of adversity. All of which make you a lot better suited to being a mom than my own mother...'

Her head swung back, and he saw her surprise, but then compassion darkened her eyes.

Why the hell had he mentioned his mom?

'So, tell me, if you want to have this baby, what are you so terrified of?' he said before she could start feeling sorry for him again.

Charley stiffened at the direct question. And the probing look in Cade's eyes.

She wished she hadn't told him about her fear, because the last thing she needed to do right now was discuss all her insecurities. Frankly, she was already freaking out enough—not least about the thought of having a link to this man for the rest of her life.

A man who scared her on a lot of levels, and not because he reminded her of her father...but because, in many ways, he didn't.

Cade was certainly ruthless and arrogant. He was also

forthright, and complex. His admission he was thrilled about this pregnancy had astonished her. It had also elated her on a visceral level.

But she knew she couldn't risk getting too invested in the way he had taken care of her this morning. Or allow his forthright defence of her character and her ability to be a good mother mean too much. All of which was no easy feat when her emotions were all over the place.

Gee, thanks, pregnancy hormones!

She placed her hand on her belly, rubbed the spot where their baby was the size of a prawn and admitted to herself she was also terrified of having to do something so important—something she wasn't convinced she would have any aptitude for—entirely alone.

What a mess...

'I just... I don't want to make a mistake,' she managed, because Cade was still watching her, waiting for a coherent answer...not that she had one to give him. 'I don't want to have this baby only to screw up its life, because I have absolutely no clue what I'm doing.'

He nodded, but the intense emotion which crossed his features had her heart bounding into her throat again.

'Does anyone know what the hell they're doing?' he said. 'Before they have kids?'

'I suppose not,' she said.

'Then I guess we'll just have to figure it out,' he said.

She nodded, feeling the emotion sting the backs of her eyes.

She blinked furiously, determined not to get sentimental about the *we* in that sentence.

But she couldn't help wondering about the tiny insight he'd given her into his relationship with his own mother.

Was that why he was so driven? And why he refused to shy away from this responsibility? While she was glad he seemed willing to do this with her, she was fairly sure their mostly terrible—or non-existent—relationships with their own parents were not going to make parenthood easy for either of them.

'If we're *both* gonna prepare for this new reality, though…' he interrupted her chaotic thoughts with typical pragmatism, his gaze dropping to her belly '…we have a lot of stuff to discuss.'

The massive understatement made her smile. 'Ya think?'

He let out a rough chuckle. And the anxiety in her stomach finally began to ease. A little. But as the car took the exit to the airport, she felt the exhaustion she'd been trying to suppress all morning envelop her again.

'Would it be okay if we put that conversation on hold? I'm shattered,' she managed. It made her feel like a wimp, but she needed some downtime before she agreed to anything.

Cade Landry was a forceful and demanding guy who she knew wouldn't think twice about making decisions for her and their baby if she gave him too much leeway.

He frowned, not too pleased with her request. 'Of course,' he said at last. 'By the way, I've arranged a thorough check-up first thing tomorrow morning with the West Coast's top ob-gyn, who happens to be based in Pacific Heights.'

Oh, did you, now?

She clamped down on her annoyance at his high-handedness. He was being conscientious. Not controlling. *Much*.

'Do you know if the West Coast's top ob-gyn is a woman?' she asked.

His frown deepened, as if he didn't have a clue why that would be relevant. Because...*men*!

'Yeah, I think so.'

'Great, well, I'll see her then. Thanks.'

They arrived at the hangar, where the Landry jet was waiting for them. She could hear him making the final arrangements with an assistant, but tuned out the conversation as she headed to the bedroom at the back of the plane.

He didn't join her.

She was glad he'd taken the hint. Because as she strapped herself into the bedroom's seat for take-off, the exhaustion seeped into her soul, the emotionally charged conversation in the car—as well as the demands of her pregnancy—taking their toll.

As the jet lifted into the early afternoon sunlight, and the plane banked over Manhattan, her heart rose into her throat. But as the jet levelled off, her heart remained jammed under her larynx.

It was less than five hours since she had woken up in Cade's arms. She could still feel the pulse of awareness in her core, where he had taken her last night with such urgency, such passion...and she had enjoyed every second of it.

But since then, her whole life—*both* their lives—had been turned on their heads. She pressed her palms to her stomach. And while she already felt a connection with the new life inside her, she also felt completely and utterly overwhelmed.

CHAPTER ELEVEN

'I SHOULD GO downstairs and start unpacking,' Charley managed as she stared at San Francisco's bustling waterfront—the historic splendour of the old Ferry Building and the majesty of the Bay Bridge stretching towards Oakland.

Cade's penthouse apartment towered over the city's financial district and the Embarcadero and was even more magnificent in the daylight. But it also looked just how she remembered it—luxurious, expertly designed, more than a little impersonal and almost as intimidating as the man himself.

Funny to think she'd run out of here about a month ago now, sure she would never see Cade again, and here she was looking at the same spectacular view with the baby they'd made together that night growing inside her.

Okay, stop thinking about the prawn for two seconds, or you'll freak out again.

'Your luggage is here,' he said. 'I told them to put the downstairs condo back on the rental market.'

She swung round. 'Um…when exactly did I agree to move in with you?' she managed, annoyed by the he-who-shall-be-obeyed tone she was becoming far too familiar with.

She'd had a solid sleep on the plane. While she still felt

off-kilter, she wasn't the fragile, over-emotional pushover she had been when they'd boarded his jet.

From the way he frowned—as if he couldn't quite believe she would contradict him—she knew it was way past time she started standing her ground. She might be pregnant with his baby, but that did not make her his property.

'When you spent a good ten minutes throwing up this morning,' he replied flatly.

Her cheeks burned. Trust him to bring that up. 'How is that relevant?'

Before she could follow up with all the reasons why it *so* wasn't, he had crossed the room and placed his palm on her cheek.

'Calm down, Charlotte,' he said softly, the concerned tone as disturbing as the sudden urge to lean into his hand. 'I don't want you on your own if you're sick again. That's all.'

She pulled away from his touch. But she couldn't deny the wave of emotion threatening to sweep away her perfectly valid objections to his high-handed behaviour. 'I still don't think I should move in with you,' she managed, far too aware of the needy feeling pressing down on her chest. 'This isn't even a real relationship,' she added. 'I'm just here as your stunt date for the summer.'

He tucked his hand into his pocket, but his gaze remained fixed on her. 'I think we've gone beyond that now, don't you?'

She stepped back, the tantalising aroma of woodsy cologne and soap playing havoc with her resolve now, too.

Surely this was just another example of her wacky hormones? Or was it the biology of pregnancy which seemed to make her body obsessed with the father of her child?

'I don't want to sleep with you again,' she said, although even she could hear the hesitation.

Could he see the yearning? Sense the arousal which was making her sex ache?

But he didn't call her out on the lie. 'The apartment has several guest rooms. Take your pick.'

'I... I still don't think it's a good idea.'

She would be living with him even if they weren't sleeping together. Wasn't that too intimate? What if she got suckered into thinking they were a real couple?

But then he disarmed her again. 'I want to be close by if you need me,' he said, a muscle ticking in his jaw.

'It's just morning sickness, Cade. It's perfectly normal. Most pregnant women get it,' she said, far too aware of the hole forming in her belly.

She recognised that hole, and the urge to fill it, which had made her do stupid things once.

She didn't want to be that reckless girl again, looking for approval from a guy like Cade—who she had discovered today had the unique ability to seize on her weakness and exploit it.

'I still want to keep an eye on you,' he said, the placid, persuasive tone contradicted by the fierce determination in his eyes. 'And FYI, I don't give a damn about other women. The only woman I give a damn about is you. Because you're the only one having my kid.'

She drew in a careful breath. The curt statement struck at the heart of her insecurities...but also made her aware of something important.

This is about his baby. It's not about you.

She took a moment to control the wayward emotions which were way too close to the surface. Again.

What if this feeling of vulnerability, this urge to accept the support he was offering, was nothing to do with that needy, unloved girl—and everything to do with the strange situation they found themselves in? If that were the case, would it be so terrible to let him carry some of the burden? To let go of a little of her independence? As long as he understood that accepting his support did not mean he could dictate her life?

'I'm pregnant, Cade. I'm not an invalid,' she said. 'I still plan to set up a workshop while I'm here to work on my commissions. My business is important to me. Especially as I'm going to be a single parent in eight months' time.'

His gaze darkened. 'You won't need to support yourself. I've asked my legal team to draw up a financial agreement which will ensure my child will never want for anything. I also intend to compensate you generously for your role as its mother. I would never abandon that responsibility.'

She sighed, her panic and confusion downgrading considerably in the face of his rigid expression—and the shadow in his eyes. She'd triggered something she hadn't intended to, but she was glad she had.

From the little he had let slip about his past, she knew Cade had some trust issues. She understood what that was like—because she had several trust issues of her own.

Living with him scared her on a lot of levels. She couldn't allow herself to need his care or his attention too much. But maybe she should do the mature thing and start dealing with how scared that made her feel before she tried to deal with his insecurities too.

'I don't want your money, Cade,' she began.

'Well, tough,' he interrupted her. 'Because there is no way in hell I'm not supporting my own child.'

She put up her palm. '*Whoa...* That's not what I said. I said *I* don't want your money. We can certainly agree on a financial arrangement between us as parents for the up-keep of our baby. When it's born.' She placed her palm on her stomach and waited for the stupid wave of emotion to level out. It was good he was so determined to support this baby. His protective instincts and sense of responsibility didn't have to be a bad thing, as long as they established some boundaries—such as that *her* life and autonomy, and their baby's well-being, were two separate issues.

'But it's not a baby yet. It's barely an embryo,' she con-tinued. 'My financial independence is important to me. I love my business. I want to make a success of Trouble Maker. You said you'd give my business your financial support while I'm here—as a trade-off for posing as your date. And I plan to hold you to that. But that's the only fi-nancial support I want from you.'

She could see the enormity of the mountain she had to climb though when his frown deepened.

Good grief, what on earth had he expected her to do while she was here? Sit around and twiddle her thumbs while he took charge of everything? Simply because she was pregnant?

She wanted to be angry with him, but had she created this rod for her own back by being so flaky over the last twelve hours?

Lesson to self: no more wimping out around Cade, no matter how crap you feel.

The thought was strangely motivating. She was bound to be tired from time to time—but she could remedy that by sleeping as much and as often as she needed to.

She had no idea how long the nausea was supposed to

last—or what other symptoms she might be dealing with in future, other than a hyperactive libido every time she was within ten feet of her child's father. Because she had completely zoned out when Dr Ramirez had given them both the lowdown on the first trimester of pregnancy that morning.

No wonder Cade thought she couldn't hold up her end of this when she'd allowed him to take the lead on everything so far. Well, that ended now.

'I don't want you working if you're sick,' he said, his voice tight with irritation.

Well, that's not your decision.

It was what she wanted to say, but she swallowed the provocative reply.

He had to be struggling, too, with the enormity of what they were dealing with. Not just logistically, but also emotionally. But she suspected from his closed expression and what she knew of him already that he would rather cut off his tongue than admit it.

Cade was a guy who she doubted ever admitted a weakness. And who always wanted to be in charge, hence his desire to wrap her in cotton wool, rather than treat her as an equal… But what if that was a lay-over from his childhood, too, a way to avoid dealing with any messy emotions?

Well, he'd have to deal with them eventually. And her. And living in his apartment with him would give her ample opportunity to find out a lot more about his fears and insecurities too.

Until then, though, she could cut him some slack. Up to a point.

'How about we compromise. I can live here with you…' She puffed out a breath. 'In the guest room,' she added hastily, when his eyes darkened with something which only made her more aware of the heat pulsing insistently in her abdomen. 'But I continue to work on my commissions during the day, and I set up my workspace in the Embarcadero as planned.'

His piercing blue eyes narrowed. She could see he didn't want to give an inch.

'Or...' she continued, determined to make him see reason. 'I get a flight back to the UK tomorrow morning...' *Two can play the carrot and stick game.* 'And we forget all about the stunt dating. And you lose the Helberg bet. Your choice.'

His frown became catastrophic. She wondered if she'd pushed him too far. But she refused to back down. Surely he couldn't still carry out his threat of suing her over those photos? Not when he was so adamant about protecting the mother of his child? So she had him, and he knew it, but it might take him a while to figure it out...

Luckily, she was more than willing to wait.

Cade was so furious he felt as if steam was about to explode out of his ears. But far worse was the heat in his groin. And that unsteady, unsettled feeling in his gut.

The same damn feeling he'd always had when he'd been yanked out of one home to be dumped in another. He had always hated the loss of control, more than the not knowing where he would wind up next. Some of the foster homes had been great, some just okay, some not even that, but in each new place he'd learned to add another layer of I-don't-give-a-damn until it hadn't mattered to him any more how good or bad the homes were, because he knew he would survive regardless. And he had promised himself that as soon as he was old enough, he would get out of the system—and finally be able to live his life on his own terms.

But as he glared at Charlotte, it occurred to him that having a baby with her was going to mean losing some of that precious control…unless he could find a way to make her play ball.

The fact that winning the bet, even acquiring Helberg, didn't mean as much to him as keeping her and the baby safe only made the whole situation more infuriating. He couldn't afford to care *too* much, because he didn't trust her not to use that weakness against him.

He couldn't deny, though, as she stood in front of him, her arms folded, her stance stubborn and determined, that being bested by her was also kind of…well, hot.

How had she managed to turn the tables on him so neatly? Because no one did that. Not any more…

Then again, everything about her was a turn-on.

Of course, he wasn't about to tell her that, because she had too much power already.

He wasn't sure how she had sneaked under his guard. But this fierce need would pass, once they'd finally got the chemical reaction they shared out of their systems. So the no sex rule was a problem. Then again, no way would they be able to keep their hands off each other for a whole five weeks while they were living in the same apartment.

'You're damn sneaky, too, when you want to be,' he said, unable to keep the admiration out of his voice.

He hated to be beaten, *ever*. But who would have guessed this poor little rich girl would have the backbone of a Trojan and the tactical smarts of a five-star general…or that he would find the challenge she represented not just infuriating, but also compelling?

She sent him a quick grin, full of relief and no small amount of triumph. The pleasure she derived from her victory turned her green eyes to a rich emerald.

'I'm going to take that as a compliment,' she said.

He hadn't intended it as one. But even so, he found himself smiling back.

'Do we have a deal?' she asked.

'I guess,' he said, forced to concede she had won this round. *Mostly.*

But as she walked by him, he yanked his hand out of his pants pocket. 'How about we shake on it?'

Her gaze darted to his. But she took his hand—because she was way too overconfident.

Big mistake.

He felt her tremble of reaction as his fingers closed around hers and his thumb caressed the rabbiting pulse in her wrist.

She yanked her hand free—sent him a quelling look, telling him she knew exactly what he had been up to with that wrist stroke. Then marched off to check out the guest rooms.

But his smile spread as he watched her go.

Yeah, you can run again, sugar, but you can't hide— not from me and sure as heck not from this chemistry. Not for long anyhow.

CHAPTER TWELVE

One week later

'CADE, YOU'RE HERE!' Charley stared at the man standing with his back to her in the huge open-plan kitchen area of the equally massive penthouse apartment they had been sharing for seven days. The man she had been managing to avoid for all seven of those days by getting back before him each evening from the workshop she was establishing a block away, and heading straight to her bedroom—because she was way too exhausted to socialise. Or eat a meal with him.

Dressed in a simple white T-shirt—which stretched distractingly over broad shoulders, a muscular back and a lean waist and dropped just shy of his equally impressive butt showcased in faded jeans—he looked relaxed and at home... The casual clothing reminded her uncomfortably of the jeans and tee combo he had looked so delicious in at the Broussards' party.

So delicious, they'd ended up creating a baby.

He turned slowly, and she spotted the meat mallet in his hand.

'Are you cooking?' she asked, stunned.

It was barely six, and the man was a workaholic. She

hadn't even realised he knew where the kitchen was, because the steel-and-marble space had remained spotless and unused—despite the groceries he'd had his assistant stock the fridge with the day after they arrived.

That would be the day when they had had their last proper conversation. Or rather their last disagreement. Because he had wanted to accompany her to the ob-gyn appointment that morning, and she had point-blank refused.

He had been annoyed, but to her surprise, he'd backed off without much of a protest. And she'd hardly seen or spoken to him since, because he left before she woke each morning and didn't return until nightfall.

Truth be told, she had been beyond grateful to be left to her own devices for the past week. Her life—and their relationship—were confusing enough without dealing with the simmering sexual tension which was always there when she was in the same room with Cade.

He had texted her each day, usually a curt line to ask her if there had been any nausea. But luckily that one episode in New York seemed to be the worst of her morning sickness over with, after her new ob-gyn, Dr Chen, had given her lots of tips on how to avoid a recurrence—as well as a ton of different vitamins to take.

Apart from ensuring his 'people' were on hand to help her with setting up her workspace—and dealing with the insane amount of paperwork necessary to hire the two brilliant seamstresses she had found—Cade had made no demands on her socially, as per their fake dating agreement. Nor had he insisted on spending any time with her in the evenings—after checking in on her when he arrived back from his office.

But as he put the mallet down on the chopping board,

and she saw the two thick steaks lined up on the counter next to an enormous array of fresh salad ingredients, she realised her reprieve was over.

'I wanted to catch you tonight before you hid out in the bedroom,' he said.

'Hid out? What is that supposed to mean?' she protested. 'I've been tired. It's hard work setting up a business and being pregnant...' she added, but before she could get up to full steam, he lifted his hand.

'Let me rephrase. Before you crashed out in the *guest* room.'

The emphasis on *guest* seemed significant, but she didn't get the chance to question what he meant by the inference before he ploughed on, cutting her outrage off at the knees. 'I've done some reading on what's best to eat during pregnancy...'

He had?

She couldn't quite hide her surprise. Or the press of something wrapping around her ribs. She'd been making the effort to eat regularly and often, as per the doctor's orders, but she hadn't had the time or inclination to cook for herself.

'Apparently bland and packed with vitamins and protein is a good call—so I figured steak, a baked potato and a side salad would work.'

'You're going to cook a meal for me?' It was a silly question, as he'd just said as much, but even so she felt the wall of emotion hit her unawares.

'Yes.'

'Oh,' she said, blinking as ridiculous tears stung her eyes.

It was just the pregnancy hormones making her over-

emotional. She'd already established that. She brushed the
moisture away with her fist, but then he tilted his head to
one side, scrutinising her in that way he had which made
her feel seen.

And the wave of emotion crested again.

'Hey, now…' He walked around the counter, clearly
as disturbed by her over-the-top reaction as she was. 'My
cooking isn't that bad, I swear.'

She found herself laughing and crying at the same time.

He brushed her tears away with his thumbs, his gaze
unguarded for the first time. But the fierce concern only
made her feel more vulnerable. And more scared.

'It's just the pregnancy hormones,' she murmured, stepping away from his gentle touch and wiping her eyes—feeling desperately exposed and pathetically needy.

'Uh-huh,' he said, but she could see the question in his
eyes.

'They hit me unawares sometimes,' she added. 'And
make me overreact to anything even remotely triggering.
Sorry.' That had to be it. She'd persuaded herself over the
past week that her initial panic about relying on Cade too
much didn't apply. This wasn't about who she'd been, but
who she was now. And as she'd started to come to terms
with the reality of the pregnancy, she had become more convinced that it made sense to lean on him, at least where the
baby was concerned. So why did this feel like too much?

'There's no need to apologise,' he said, but then he
added, 'Why would you be triggered by me cooking for
you?'

She sighed. She didn't want to answer. Because it felt
too personal. And if she told him the truth, too revealing.

But she could see she'd been a coward in the past week.

She *had* been hiding out in her room, avoiding him. One of the reasons why she'd decided to stay here was to get to know him better, to deal with a few of his insecurities too, and discover what kind of a father he would be.

But didn't that require conversation? Time spent together, talking openly?

There were so many things she wanted to know about him—about his past, his childhood, the things which kept him up at night, which drove him so relentlessly, even the reason why acquiring Helberg seemed so important to him. But if she wanted him to reveal his secrets, his vulnerabilities—then she had to be willing to do the same.

'I guess because no one has ever cooked a meal for me before—well, not like this,' she offered.

'I see,' he said. He didn't seem all that surprised—maybe no one had ever cooked a meal for him either. But the thought made her consider how tough his childhood must have been in comparison to hers, and she found herself backtracking.

'Which is, of course, nonsense, now I think about it. Even though he ignored me, my father paid a small fortune to the staff when I was little to make sure I was well cared for while my mother was alive. Then I went to a string of expensive boarding schools—with a host of catering options. And the last thing you want when you're a catwalk model is to have someone cook you a meal before a show...' She began babbling, because his scrutiny had only become more intense. 'Just in case you gain a couple of millimetres on your hips and can't get into the designs assigned to you. So apparently, the pregnancy hormones are making me feel sorry for myself for no reason.'

He frowned. 'I'm not sure having someone paid to care

for your needs or being forced to starve yourself counts as no reason,' he murmured. Then he threw her completely by asking, 'What happened to your mother?'

'She died when I was eight,' she said.

'That's tough,' he said, his gaze darkening with sympathy.

'Not particularly. We were never close. She spent most of my childhood living at the family estate in Northumberland while I lived with my father in London. And she was so unhappy. She just wasn't ever really *there* even when she was, if you know what I mean… So when she took her own life, I didn't feel the loss. Not the way Adam did.'

'But you were just a little kid. Even when your mama isn't around, it still hurts when they're gone,' he said, his gaze filled with a compassion she knew must come from his own experiences.

She seized on the small insight. 'When did you lose your mother?'

His gaze became instantly shuttered before he gave a harsh laugh, devoid of humour. 'I didn't lose her. She lost me.'

'How do you mean?' she asked.

His expression went carefully blank. 'She left me in a department store in Baton Rouge when I was five years old. Told me to hide out and she'd come back to get me. So I did, until the nightwatchman found me the next morning and called the cops.' He shrugged, but the movement lacked his usual grace. 'And that's how I got kicked into the system.'

Charlotte touched his hand, her heart racing—the lack of emotion in his voice and his blank expression only making

his story sadder. It wasn't hard to see where Cade's trust issues came from now. 'Cade, I'm so sorry. That's dreadful.'

'Not really. She was a junkie. I was better off without
her.'

'Even so, no child should have no one,' she said, the emotion threatening to overwhelm her again. No matter how
unseen she'd sometimes felt as a child, however much of a
burden she'd been made to feel, she had never been alone.
Some of the staff and teachers paid to care for her had been
kind and nurturing, and she had always had Adam. However dysfunctional their relationship had been at times, he
had always been there for her in a crisis.

'I wasn't alone. I had myself,' he said as he skimmed
his thumb under her eye. 'Please don't start crying again.'

She laughed and sniffed back the tears, stupidly relieved
all of a sudden. She'd been so terrified of relying on him
too much, but surely sharing the burden together could be
mutual? It didn't have to leave her overexposed. If he was
exposed too.

Before she could probe further, though, he lifted her
bag off her shoulder and slung an arm around her waist to
direct her towards the kitchen's breakfast counter. 'Take a
load off while I finish supper.'

He'd changed the conversation deliberately. Clearly, getting him to talk about his past was going to be a work in
progress, but she felt deeply moved by what he'd shared.
And once she'd climbed up on the stool and managed to
tamp down on the inevitable buzz of awareness from that
proprietary touch, watching him cook her dinner was captivating too.

She gave herself permission to enjoy the moment and
not overthink it.

He worked quickly and efficiently, slicing the salad ingredients with the speed and skill of a chef.

'Where did you learn to chop so fast?' she asked.

He glanced up. 'I worked as a short-order cook in a diner while doing my MBA at Yale,' he said. 'I had a couple of scholarships to cover tuition, but I was already investing the money I'd earned flipping houses into building a property portfolio, so working the breakfast and the late shifts in between the classes and assignments kept me afloat.'

'When did you sleep?' she asked, astonished. Surely the workload at Yale's renowned business school would have been enormous enough? 'And socialise?'

'I didn't do either, much.' He sent her a wry smile as he fired up the griddle. 'You don't need all that much sleep in your early twenties. And I've always been a loner, with a passionate aversion to small talk,' he added by way of explanation while pulling two jacket potatoes covered in tin foil from the oven.

'Have you always worked this hard then?' she asked, fascinated.

The man wasn't so much a workaholic as a work machine... But his drive and ambition—and almost preternatural focus on getting what he wanted—suddenly seemed as hot as the scent of his woodsy cologne, and the sight of his biceps bulging beneath the short sleeves of his T-shirt as he hammered out the steaks.

She shifted on the stool. *Fabulous*. Even watching him cook aroused her.

'I guess.' He shrugged as he set the steaks on the hot griddle. 'It's not difficult to motivate yourself, though, when you love what you do.'

Plus, hard work was the only way to make your mark

if you came from nothing, the way he had. It was a sober-ing thought.

She loved what she did too, now. And she'd worked ex-tremely hard to get her business operational. The chal-lenges she'd faced in the last few days as she interviewed seamstresses, organised for Landry Construction to em-ploy them to comply with her visa status, and began work on her newest commissions had been frustrating and time-consuming but also exhilarating. What she had achieved already with Trouble Maker meant so much more to her than being able to look elegant prancing down a catwalk without falling on her bum!

But she'd never had the sustained focus he had, and she'd never been reliant on herself alone to survive and prosper. She could see that more clearly now.

'How do you like your steak?' he asked, breaking her out of her revelry and making her aware of her stomach grum-bling from the delicious scent of sizzling meat.

'Medium rare is good,' she said.

She watched him as he finished off the meal—splitting the potatoes, adding generous amounts of butter and sour cream and chives, tossing the salad in a dressing he rustled up from scratch, and flipping the steaks. By the time he'd finished, she felt oddly humbled and stupidly emotional again. And hopelessly turned on.

Cade Landry might be arrogant, and overwhelming, and cynical, and tightly controlled when it came to his emotions as well as his work ethic—but all those things also made him exciting and fascinating…and really hot.

'Dig in,' he said as he placed the loaded plates on the breakfast bar and climbed onto the stool across from her.

She didn't have to be asked twice. She cut into the per-

fectly cooked steak, put it in her mouth and let the meaty
juices dissolve on her tongue.

'Delicious,' she moaned.

'Yeah,' he said, his gaze roaming over her in a way that
made her skin tingle.

The sweet spot between her thighs—which only he had
ever found—rejoiced right alongside her taste-buds. She
stiffened, acknowledging the danger. Apparently, Cade
Landry's culinary skills were as seductive as all his other
skills....

They ate in silence. She polished off most of the enormous steak and made inroads into the potato and crisp
salad. But once he had cleared his plate, she was forced
to admit defeat.

'You done?' he asked.

'Yes, thanks, it was very good,' she said as he scooped
up the plates, cleaned the remnants of her meal into the
waste disposal and loaded the dinnerware into a state-of-
the-art dishwasher.

'So, I think I'll head to bed,' she said, trying to lessen
the sexual tension threatening to devour her almost as efficiently as he had demolished his steak.

Because watching the man do domestic chores was stupidly sexy, too. Who knew?

The confidences they'd shared about their pasts, their
childhoods—and the fact they had both, in different ways,
been abandoned by their mothers—threatened a level of
intimacy which she needed to process before she did anything daft.

This still wasn't a real relationship. She had to remember
that. He'd only offered her more than the other women he'd

dated because she carried his child. An accidental conception didn't make them a couple.

But as she got off the stool to head to her bedroom, the delicious steak she had devoured now sitting like a brick in her stomach—her emotions churning right under it—he strode around the kitchen counter and snagged her arm.

'Wait up, Charlotte.' He tugged her around to face him. 'Don't run out on me again,' he said, and she heard the tension. 'This doesn't have to be a stunt relationship, not when we both want each other so much.'

He rested a hand on her hip.

She could move away from him, tell him she didn't want him with the same urgency, the same need. But how could she? When her sex was already aching to be filled. The need to protect herself from any romantic delusions, though, was still paramount.

'I'm not sure that's smart,' she said.

'Why not?' he asked as emotion swirled in his eyes.

Because I'm still a little scared I could end up needing you too much.

She pushed the terrifying thought away this time. One thing she'd always been was a realist. Even as a little girl. He wasn't offering love, and she didn't want it. Because that would leave her more vulnerable, and she was vulnerable enough already.

'I'm scared of becoming a burden or a responsibility,' she said.

And wanting something I can't have.

That was how she'd always felt as a child. Because of the mother who had been too sick to acknowledge her, the father who had never cared about anyone but himself. And the big brother who had treated her for so much of their lives as a duty to be managed.

Cade swore softly, still holding his hand on her hip his body vibrating now with the same frustration she felt.

'That's not how I see you, Charlotte. You're witty and vibrant and infuriating and sexy as hell. I don't want to take your independence away from you... But I've gotta tell you, living here with you, knowing my kid is growing inside you and being unable to touch you, is driving me nuts.'

She lifted her head and looked into his eyes. She saw the need and the passion which matched her own. And felt herself melting.

'You can touch me, Cade. I *want* you to touch me. As long as we're clear that's all this is. Nothing more than an itch we both enjoy scratching.'

He cradled her cheek, and she saw the flash of triumph—the aching desire. And felt oddly hollow inside.

But she knew she had to stand firm.

She had been broken before, in so many ways. Whatever happened, she had to prevent herself from being broken again—but she could do that as long as they set out clear parameters for this relationship.

'Understood,' he said, his hand stroking her neck, his thumb toying with the thundering pulse in her collarbone. 'But I want you in my bed, not the damn guest room.'

She nodded. She could give him that—it was the practical, grown-up solution.

Giving in to this raw, insistent need was dangerous. She understood that. But physical intimacy was only that, and as long as she understood this, surely it didn't have to derail her emotionally...

'Yes, okay.'

Before she had got the words out, he boosted her into his arms.

She wrapped her legs around his waist and pressed her mouth to those hard, sensual lips as he carried her into the bedroom they had shared once before… The bedroom where their baby had been created. But as she bared her body to him, she promised herself she would never bare her soul.

CHAPTER THIRTEEN

Two weeks later

CADE GROANED, clinging to his sanity, the pleasure threatening to burst through his veins like wildfire as he thrust heavily into Charlotte, barely aware of the power shower thundering down on them both.

Not yet. Not yet. Hold on.

His mind blurred, his knees trembling, his fingers digging into her hips as he held them both upright with the last of his strength, adjusting his thrusts to stroke the spot inside her he knew would take her over.

Her body tightened on his, her sob of surrender triggering his own orgasm as he crashed over at last. He groaned, the climax intensifying as he sank his face into her wet hair, drowning in brutal sensation. *Again.*

How could their chemistry still be so damn strong? So damn frantic? When they'd been making love like rabbits for two weeks straight. Every morning, every evening and any stolen moment in between...

He stood, letting the vicious afterglow wash over him, only vaguely aware of the water jets still pummelling his back. Until she shifted, reviving from the titanic orgasm first.

'We should get out of here before we dissolve,' she murmured.

He let out a rough chuckle. And how could she still captivate him? When he'd been living with her for three weeks?

Shouldn't he be bored by now? Eager to consider other living arrangements?

She was over the morning sickness, hadn't had an episode since that first one in New York. She didn't need him to watch over her so closely.

But not only couldn't he keep his hands off her in the bedroom—and everywhere else in the apartment, even the damn kitchen counter yesterday evening—he had become addicted to her company, too.

They ate together each evening now, and although her attempts to pry more details out of him about his past had started to become problematic, he'd deflected them by exploiting their voracious appetite for one another whenever she got too close. It was bad enough she knew the truth about his mother. He didn't want her to know any more.

Luckily, their lovemaking gave him an easy out from the probing queries, the questions he had no intention of answering…and in the last few days, she'd stopped asking them.

But that wasn't the only cause for concern.

He found it next to impossible now not to return from work early—or surprise her at her workspace in the Ferry Building so he could escort her back to the apartment in the evenings—because he enjoyed spending time with her so much. He loved hearing about the latest news on her commissions, checking out the designs she was working on—not that he knew a damn thing about haute couture. Her enthusiasm was captivating, and he was proud of what she'd achieved in such a short space of time.

'Water off,' he demanded, grateful for the voice-activated controls. Then lifted her from him.

She left the cubicle, and he took the opportunity to check out the subtle changes caused by her pregnancy before she had wrapped a towel around her naked body.

Her breasts had become fuller and more sensitive, and although he couldn't see a bump yet, her waist had thickened slightly. Although that could be the food he'd been feeding her every chance he got. Charlotte had a voracious appetite for his cooking too, and he loved to watch her eat.

But what he enjoyed more was the surprise on her face when he made the effort for her.

Kind of weird, because he'd never been a nurturer, but he couldn't seem to shake the feeling of connection. Their upbringings couldn't have been more different—but in many ways they'd survived the same loss. When she'd talked about losing her mama too, the vulnerability on her face had stirred something inside him he couldn't explain.

However wealthy her folks had been, she had grown up without their emotional support. But while he'd built a wall around himself so he didn't need the validation of anyone but himself, he sensed she had never done that.

It made him ashamed for having once dismissed her as spoilt and entitled when she'd been the opposite. But her open, generous nature also made him wary. Was he becoming too dependent on her company? That kinetic connection? The spectacular chemistry? Should he be weaning himself off her before her pregnancy became more pronounced? He couldn't afford to get suckered into needing anyone. He'd been there as a kid, and it had nearly destroyed him.

He strolled out of the shower, feeling the familiar throb

of awareness when her gaze skimmed over him. Colour heightened her cheeks as she looked away again.

'I should probably head to the other bathroom to get ready for tonight,' she said, all business. 'What's the dress code again?'

'Smart casual, I guess,' he said, trying to remember what event it was and why he had accepted the invitation—when all he wanted to do right now was have her again.

He hooked a towel around his waist, but when she headed past him, he grabbed her hand. 'We don't have to go if you're tired.'

She blushed, then smiled—the dazzling smile which always made his heartbeat slow.

'Hmm…' she said, stroking her chin like a professor discovering the meaning of life. 'Is that a Landry euphemism for "Why don't I jump you again so I can tire you out even more?"'

He tugged her into his arms, enjoying the way she always challenged him, the hunger increasing. 'You got me,' he murmured.

'Not gonna happen, Galahad,' she said, dancing free, still smiling provocatively. She took a few more steps back as she wrapped the towel tighter. 'This is another great opportunity to show off one of my creations, which I am not about to throw away because you are completely insatiable. So have a cold shower and I'll see you in the lobby in twenty looking fabulous.'

He swore under his breath, really wishing he hadn't accepted the invite. He didn't want to share her for the rest of the evening with anyone.

He forced himself to ignore the thought.

The plan—such as it was—had never been to keep her

forever. It was time he started getting a handle on this ob-session.

But as she walked away, the yearning gripped his chest regardless. And it occurred to him it was going to be a lot harder than he had ever thought it would be to let her go. Eventually.

She turned at the door.

'Changed your mind?' he quipped.

'Nope,' she said despite the flush of arousal. 'I forgot to tell you. My first sonogram is next week. Dr Chen has scheduled it for the Friday before Labor Day. I thought...' She hesitated, panic stabbed under his breastbone.

'Is there a problem?' Was there something she wasn't telling him? 'With the baby?'

'Oh, no, not at all,' she said. Relief made him feel light-headed as she continued. 'I just thought you might like to put it in your diary...so you can come, too.'

He opened his mouth ready to say he'd be there. He wanted to see the life growing inside her. He'd thought about it often, especially late at night, when she was sleep-ing and the thoughts he couldn't control bombarded him.

Would his child—*their* child—be a boy or a girl? Would it have her charisma? His drive? What would they call it?

But right alongside those thoughts had been the yearning which he recognised from long ago. The desire to belong, to be a part of a family, to have someone care for him, the way his own mother never had. The yearning which had never been fulfilled. And could destroy him if he gave in to it again.

With that yearning came the memory of fear and panic, the scent of floor cleaner and the gentle voice of the guard asking, *Where are your folks, boy?*

He swallowed the knee-jerk answer and took a mental step back.

'You sure that's smart?' he asked, trying to think of a viable excuse not to go. 'We don't want to get photographed going into an obstetric clinic together. Because that would reignite the press attention we don't want.'

'I see your point,' Charley said carefully. Even though she didn't.

It had taken her days to mention the appointment to him. Because she wanted so desperately for him to come. But she had been waiting for an opportunity to mention it, and it hadn't materialized.

Cade never willingly spoke about the baby.

She'd tried to convince herself that was normal. That men probably didn't really connect with their baby until it felt more tangible to them, more real.

And he seemed invested in the pregnancy itself—insisting on cooking nutritious and delicious meals for her. And always asking her how she was feeling. She'd noticed the careful way he caressed her breasts when they made love, aware of how sensitive they had become. And she loved the possessive way he rested his palm on her belly, where their baby grew, when he thought she was asleep.

So many times she had wanted to turn over and ask him what he was feeling, what he was thinking. But she'd held back, scared to risk breaking cover. All her old insecurities told her she might not get the answer she wanted, so it was better not to ask.

They had time, lots of time to deal with the reality of becoming parents before the baby arrived. They'd only been together for three weeks, and they weren't a couple in the traditional sense.

But despite all those careful qualifications, her determination not to let his reticence bother her, she could feel the chill running through her at his blank expression now.

For a moment there, she'd seen the flicker of excitement in the deep blue of his irises. And hope had blossomed like a flower in her chest. Why had she been such a coward about telling him? Why had she avoided talking about the baby, too?

But the excitement had disappeared so swiftly, she wasn't sure if she had imagined it.

She didn't want to be needy, to seem insecure. Things were good between them. Things were great. In many ways they'd become friends as well as lovers in the last few weeks.

She loved it when he touched her. Adored indulging the raw passion. But she found his attention even more intoxicating. She looked forward now to the conversations they shared each evening. He'd shown genuine interest in her business—and had offered her some invaluable advice, while also escorting her to numerous events which would give her creations exposure.

But she couldn't contain her dismay at his reasoning now. The press attention which had forced them together in the first place had died down a lot in the last month. Ever since they'd appeared at the High Line event together, the media had lost interest and moved on to the next big celebrity scandal… After all, Cade Landry wasn't a one date wonder any more, and she wasn't a wild child. Now they had shacked up together.

'The media could just as easily photograph me going to the clinic on my own. And put two and two together,' she said, deciding to press. She didn't want him being prevented from this seminal moment in their baby's life because of something which was unlikely to happen. 'But anyway, the only time we've been photographed recently is at public events. I don't think we're much of a story any more.'

'I guess,' he said, but she could still see the reluctance in his eyes.

Maybe she was making a big deal about nothing? Whether he came to the scan or not didn't have to mean anything. Perhaps his reluctance to attend the appointment really was just about logistics.

And anyhow, why did it matter how involved he wanted to be at this point? They were still months and months away from the birth. They hadn't even spoken yet about where she would be living when that happened. In theory, she would be back in the UK. But that was another conversation she'd avoided.

'How about you let me think about it,' he said carefully. 'I've got to be in Manhattan on Labor Day itself. And I may have to head to the East Coast a couple days ahead of schedule.'

'No problem.' She forced herself to smile. The jaunty I'm-all-right-Jack smile she'd perfected as a child whenever her mother looked right through her as if she wasn't there. 'I'll see you in twenty, then,' she said, and fled.

But as she retreated to the guest room—where she kept the array of designs for the public appearances they made—and put together a suitable outfit, she didn't feel her usual excitement about showing off her work. And when they arrived at the exclusive garden party in the Presidio, and her hand rested on Cade's forearm as he led her into the event, she felt the bitter pang of loneliness she remembered from so much of her childhood, even though he was right beside her.

CHAPTER FOURTEEN

One week later

'CADE, YOU MADE IT!'

'Yeah, I managed to get out of the meeting early.' Cade strolled into the obstetrician's waiting area. Guilt twisted in his gut, though, at the pleasure—and relief—in Charlotte's expression.

He hadn't intended to come. He'd lined up a ton of excuses over the past week—ever since she'd mentioned the sonogram. Valid, reasonable excuses as to why he couldn't make it.

He needed to start easing himself out of this relationship. He was getting too attached. The pregnancy, and the need to protect and support his child, were getting all mixed up in his head with his feelings for the baby's mother. And his inability to stop wanting her...all the damn time.

But as he had sat in on the internet call with the zoning commissioner and his architects on a development in Monterey that afternoon, all he'd been able to think about was Charlotte having to navigate this milestone on her own—the way she'd probably had to navigate so many others alone, just like he had. As the meeting had dragged on, his attention kept straying to the clock in the corner of his screen—and the guilt had twisted into tighter and tighter knots. Until he hadn't been able to bear it any longer. And he'd cut off the debate about permits and zoning applications, shot out of the office, jumped in the nearest cab and shouted at the driver to fight through downtown traffic to get here. Just in time.

But as he sat beside her and she grasped his hand, the look on her face so bright and happy to see him there, he felt like a fraud.

'Thanks for coming, Cade. I'm so nervous,' she said.

'You are?' he asked, surprised. He knew she'd wanted him to attend the scan, but she hadn't seemed worried. 'Why?'

'I think they check for any defects, as well as all the obvious things, like if it has the beginnings of a penis,' she said, her grin spreading over her whole face as her fingers tightened on his. 'Will you want to know if they can make an educated guess?'

'A guess about what?' he asked, not able to follow the thread of the conversation, the guilt increasing.

Why was he here? When he already knew he couldn't be a part of this baby's life, not in any tangible sense. Because it would mean being a part of her life too.

'The sex, of course!' she said, just as a woman in a white coat appeared.

'Dr Chen is ready for you, Ms Courtney.' The older woman sent Cade a welcoming smile. 'And, Mr Landry. We're so glad you could make it, too.' The nurse led them through the corridors of the state-of-the-art facility, but wouldn't stop talking. 'This is always such an important moment in a parent's journey, and it's always wonderful to have both parents here to witness it.'

Parents?

The word added weight to the guilty brick in his gut.

How could he be a parent when this child could never be more than an abstract concept to a guy like him? He'd never known his own father—had guessed the guy was probably one of the other junkies in the drug dens his mother frequented, according to the social worker's report he'd unearthed, before he'd stopped looking.

Charlotte let go of his hand to get ready for the sonogram in an adjoining room. He was introduced to Dr Chen as they waited in the examination room. She asked him if he had any questions, but he could feel the panic starting to strangle him. So he shook his head and didn't ask the questions he'd thought about often in the past couple of weeks—while trying not to think about them.

Charlotte reappeared wearing a simple green gown. Her conversation with Dr Chen—detailing her current health—floated in the room around Cade as she lay down on a long couch. He rubbed clammy palms down his pants legs, aware his hands were starting to sweat. The hum of the machine opposite them powered up as the screen began to glow with an eerie blue light.

The chemical scent of the gel the doctor put on the wand she held, and the sight of Charlotte's nervous smile as Chen pressed the wand to her bare belly, only intensified the chaotic swirl of emotions pushing at the edges of Cade's consciousness.

A fast-throbbing beat—like the ticking of an overactive clock—cut through the noise in Cade's head, and a picture formed on the screen.

'There we are,' the doctor announced with a smile in her

voice. 'Junior has a nice strong heartbeat, you'll be glad to know.'

Charlotte's sharp intake of breath dragged Cade out of his trance.

'Oh, wow!' Her gaze connected with his.

The sheen of raw emotion was unguarded, and so beautiful and brave and unafraid in that moment, his own pulse accelerated to match the giddy ticking of the amplified heartbeat.

Cade forced his gaze to the screen as the doctor pointed out the spine, the head, the legs and arms, already forming. The skull looked enormous to him, the body curled in on itself. No wonder they called it the foetal position. The screen became filled with lines and dots as the doctor took what she said were essential measurements. Charlotte asked questions, most of which he couldn't make out because of the blood thundering in his ears.

He couldn't stop staring at the life they'd made together. Because of a busted condom. The life that hadn't really been real to him until this moment—except as an opportunity to put his mark on the future. And on Charlotte.

What an arrogant jerk he'd been. To think he could manage his feelings towards this tiny human being the same way he managed his businesses.

Awe swept through him, stronger even than the afterglow when he made love to Charlotte. But right behind it was the fear. And the loneliness which made the weight on his chest crush his ribs. And suddenly he was back in that department store—waking up to find himself in the dark. Alone.

'Cade, do you want to know the sex?' Charlotte's excited question pierced through the old nightmare.

'Huh?' he managed, trying to drag himself back to the present.

'Dr Chen says the baby's sex is clear enough for her to make a good guess, if we want to know. Although it's not going to be one hundred percent at this point.'

But wouldn't knowing the sex just make this *more* real?

'Whatever you want to do is good with me,' he said, struggling to cover the panic with nonchalance.

'Okay.' A frown creased Charlotte's forehead. 'Well, I've never been very patient.' She turned to the doctor. 'I'd love to know. Are we talking penis or no penis?'

The doctor laughed and then pressed the wand back into Charlotte's abdomen. She pointed at the screen. 'You see that small nub? I think we're talking the beginnings of a penis, Charley.'

A boy? He was having a son?

The rest of the appointment passed by in a daze as he attempted to keep the wave of panic at bay. He could imagine the child clearly now. But it only made the fear and insecurity worse. Because he could also see himself as a boy, his earliest memories becoming more vivid, leaping out of the place where he'd kept them locked down for so long. The scent of trash and urine, the shouts which made him cower, the darkness closing in, the nightwatchman's torch searing his eyes and dragging him from sleep into a new terrifying reality. He'd been so defenceless then. How could he protect a child when he had never even been able to protect himself?

He managed to calm his breathing, get his giddy heart rate under control as he waited for Charlotte outside the sonogram suite.

When she appeared, she looked radiant. The short summer dress she wore clung to her body, accentuating her increasingly bountiful breasts. The shot of need was familiar, but with it was something else, something he'd noticed more and more in the past few weeks—something deep and visceral and raw. And almost as terrifying as seeing his baby for the first time.

Longing.

'So, it looks like the baby is going to have a penis,' Charlotte said as she tucked her arm through his. Her voice was light, her expression full of the joy he had seen in the suite. 'How do you feel about that? Did you have a preference?'

'No,' he managed, still feeling as if he were walking through a fog.

'Is the right answer…' she said, but her eyes had lost some of their happy glow as he escorted her to his car in the parking garage below the building.

They drove through the downtown streets, his anxiety increasing as the silence he couldn't fill stretched between them.

A part of him wanted to take her back to the penthouse, to sink into her, to make her sigh and moan and shudder in his arms—so he could make this simple again.

But it had never been simple. Not with her. And that wasn't just because of the baby. It was about so much more. His emotions weren't his own. He'd lost control long before they'd made this baby. He had to get it back or he would never be able to find his safe space again. And forget about that little boy hiding in a corner and waiting for someone to find him, to want him, when no one ever had.

'Cade, what's wrong?' Charley murmured as they walked into his penthouse.

She'd absorbed his silence in the car and tried to figure

it out. But she had known something was very wrong ever since she'd come out of the dressing area at the clinic to find him waiting for her, his face ashen.

She'd been overjoyed to see him when he'd turned up for the appointment, having resigned herself to his no-show. And she'd been so happy and excited during the scan itself, especially once the doctor had declared the baby healthy. She hadn't really been aware of Cade's reaction—because she'd been so absorbed in the emotional hit of seeing the life they had created. But she was aware of it now, because it was impossible to ignore. He had looked stricken when she had found him in the waiting area. And now, it seemed as if he wasn't even here.

'I need to head to the airport,' he said.

'What?' she said, shocked by the abrupt statement and the cool tone.

'I have to be in Manhattan for Labor Day,' he replied. 'And I've got a lot to settle before then.'

'I know, but...'

Before she could say more, he had left her to walk into their bedroom.

She raced after him. 'Really, you have to go this evening?' she asked, hating the tremble of anxiety, confused now as well as shocked.

'Yeah.' He grabbed a bag from inside the dresser, began dumping clothes into it.

'Cade, is this about the sonogram? What's wrong? What happened to you in there?' she asked again, suddenly determined to face this situation head-on.

She'd thought they'd made a breakthrough this afternoon. That he was finally willing to engage with the reality of the baby instead of just the pregnancy. But why had she let him get away with his disengagement for so long? He'd wanted this baby, too. Weren't they supposed to be in this together? What was really going on here? Something about this felt hideously familiar, reminding her of all the times she'd begged her mother to see her, to respond to her, and she never had. Or tried to get her father's attention, only to be informed her feelings, her needs, really weren't important in the grand scheme of things.

He headed to the bathroom and reappeared with his hands full of his toiletries. He dumped them in the bag too, then zipped it up.

'Cade, stop!' She pressed shaking fingers over his. 'Look at me.' He lifted his head, his gaze finally meeting hers. 'What is going on? You have to tell me. You're starting to scare me...'

'Charlotte, I'm sorry,' he said, his voice so grave it only scared her more. But then he cradled her cheek, and what she saw in his eyes calmed the panic, at least a little.

Yearning. Need. Connection.

But when she leant into his palm, he dragged it away.

'You must have known,' he said, 'that this was only ever meant to be temporary.'

She heard it then, the finality, the dismissal. It cut her like a knife. And made her realise she had somehow convinced herself that this was more. That this was better. That this *could* be something. When it had always been nothing. For him, anyway.

There were so many things she could say as he slung the bag onto his shoulder.

What about the baby they shared? What about the emotions inside her which had blossomed and bloomed and grown over the past weeks every time he looked at her with such longing, such passion? Maybe even before that? Maybe right back to that night across the bay when she'd danced with him and felt truly seen for the first time in her life.

How could she have misinterpreted all of that so completely?

She felt her heart tearing and shattering, though, unable to voice any of it as he rested his hand on her abdomen and pressed a kiss to her forehead.

Tears scoured her eyes as she saw the sadness in his face.

It doesn't have to be this way. Don't leave me. Why can't you love me? Why can't I be enough?

The terror returned as the questions reverberated inside her, but she couldn't get them past the huge lump in her throat. And as he stepped back, she made herself believe she didn't want to ask the questions, because she had always known the answers, and all she had left now was her pride.

'My legal team will be in touch about the financial arrangements for the baby,' he said. 'Stay here as long as you want. The place is yours. Landry Construction will continue to pay your business expenses and all your other costs for as long as you need.'

She didn't reply. She stood stoic and unbending as she watched him leave her.

But when the lift doors closed behind him, she walked to the window, and the tears came. They streamed down her face as the choking sobs queued up in her throat.

She rested her hand on her belly, where Cade had touched her for the last time.

Stroking the place where their baby grew.

Not theirs. *Hers.*

'You're not his any more,' she whispered, out loud to

the empty apartment. 'You're mine. He doesn't want you, but I do.'

But even as she said the words, she knew a part of this baby would always be his, just like the foolish part of her heart which she'd opened to him—after convincing herself she wouldn't. After knowing she shouldn't.

The part of her heart he'd discarded all too easily.

CHAPTER FIFTEEN

Labor Day

Helberg is yours. I concede the bet. Give my best to Charley.

CADE STARED AT the text which had just appeared on his
phone from Adam Courtney as he stood in the locker room
of the club. He swiped sweat off his brow—caused by the
hour he'd just spent on the treadmill—attempting to keep
his focus on business. And not Charlotte.

In preparation for his meeting in ten minutes with her
brother to declare the winner of the bet—which now wasn't
happening.

Courtney had thrown in the towel, just like Zane a month
ago. Cade had won the bet.

He should be contacting his finance team, setting the
wheels in motion to snap up the rest of the Helberg shares.
No other viable buyers had appeared since the three of
them had made the bet on the Fourth of July. He was clear
to finish the takeover.

Helberg was his.

But instead of the elation he should be feeling, he felt
hollow. Empty. And more alone than he'd felt even as a kid
when he'd had no one.

He sat down heavily on one of the locker room benches. He could hear a couple of the other guys who were there on a vacation day, talking about Cornell's college football team and their chances for the new season, the showers running, a nineties rap anthem playing on the speakers.

But all he could really hear was Charlotte and the last words she'd said to him—hopelessness and confusion in her voice.

What is going on? You have to tell me. You're starting to scare me.

So he'd told her. Not the whole truth, but enough of the truth so she would know he couldn't be a parent. He couldn't even be a partner to her.

And it seemed like she'd got the message, because she hadn't contacted him in the days since.

Give my best to Charley.

The offhand comment in Courtney's text seared his brain. Dating Charlotte had won him Helberg. Weird, it hadn't even occurred to him until this moment that she had given him this victory.

Give it up, man. This is what you wanted, what you worked for. All these years. You can't go back and change who you are, who you've become for her...or for the baby.

He forced himself to switch the phone on and texted his EA. His fingers shaking.

Tell finance to finish the Helberg buyout.

But as he switched the phone off and headed into the showers, the sense of triumph, the validation he should have been feeling, never came. And the hollow ache in his gut became a black hole.

Four days later

Charley stared up at the stunning Art Deco tower which housed the Courtney Collection as the cab she'd taken from the airport sped back into the afternoon traffic. Twenty-five storeys of luxury, elegance, and class, with her brother Adam's penthouse offices at the top.

Funny to think she'd never visited him here. Just another example of what a coward she'd always been. The truth was, she really didn't want to be here now. She felt so fragile and wounded and pathetic, and it wasn't as if she and Adam had ever had a particularly close relationship.

But in amongst all the heartache and recriminations she'd been heaping on herself over the past week—as she wound up her workshop in San Francisco, said goodbye to Rachel and Lanisha, her brilliant seamstresses, and worked out the logistics of her relocation back to East London—she'd realised she owed her brother an apology.

According to the reports of Landry Construction's historic takeover of Helberg Holdings—which had been all over the business news for two days—Cade had won the bet. Which meant he now owned Montague's, the jewellery company Adam had been so desperate to buy back.

She had arranged a twelve-hour stop-over in New York en route to the UK to say she was sorry to her brother.

As she introduced herself to the receptionist in the extravagant lobby area—where a towering wall of glass separated the refined elegance of the interior from the manic energy of Madison Avenue during the lunch hour—it occurred to her that her brother might not even be here.

Her hopes were dashed, though, when the perfectly made-up receptionist contacted his PA and directed her to a bank of lifts, stating Adam would see her straight away.

Her heart plummeted along with her stomach as the lift climbed up the building. The scrape of tears which she refused to shed—because she'd shed more than enough of them already—made her throat feel raw.

Her mind started to wander to yet more devastating what-ifs as she was directed into the private penthouse office's double-height space by a friendly woman called Maggie who had met her at the lift on the floor below. Here too, the glass added so much light her eyes stung. She'd spent a good twenty minutes doing her make up on the flight from San Francisco, though, so hopefully Adam wouldn't notice the results of her week-long crying jag.

But what if she owed him more than an apology? Would he expect an explanation for why she'd dated Cade Landry for over a month—and then been dropped like a stone?

She covered her belly.

Should she tell him about the baby? She wasn't really showing yet, but they were siblings after all. And he was going to become an uncle…of the son of the man who had robbed him of Montague's.

She was swallowing rapidly, trying to get a handle on the latest wave of panic and misery—when her brother appeared on the mezzanine level and jogged down the steps to meet her.

'Charley? This is a surprise?' he said, but he didn't sound angry with her, weirdly. 'I certainly hope you didn't bring that bastard Landry with you.'

She jolted slightly before she noticed he was smiling, his expression relaxed. The joke only made her feel smaller and more insignificant, though. And hopeless.

She blinked rapidly, trying to hold back more self-indulgent tears. But as he got closer, his eyes narrowed, and he frowned.

'Charley, what's wrong?' he said with a perceptiveness which threw her back in time, to a memory from long ago. A memory she realised she'd forgotten until this moment. Of standing and staring hopelessly at the broken earth of her mother's grave while shivering uncontrollably in the cold March wind. Until Adam had taken her hand and squeezed her chilled fingers. And made the shuddering stop.

He was looking at her now the same way—with concern, with understanding, with support.

The choking weight rose up her chest, and a sob lurched out of her mouth. The stinging tears scoured her throat, and the mask of competence and capability she'd been faking desperately for days collapsed...

She started shaking, not aware of what he was saying as he wrapped his arm around her shoulders. He held her close as the misery poured out of her and onto his clean white shirt. The flood of pain, of humiliation, was nothing though compared to the deep sense of loss.

But how can you lose something you never had?

His soothing words were gruff, but gentle and surprisingly not at all judgemental. At last, the raging storm of grief passed, and she became aware of the comforting scent of laundry detergent which clung to him. And the weight of his arm on her shoulder as he sat beside her.

How had they ended up on the couch? She didn't even know.

He handed her a tissue from the dispenser on the coffee table. 'Okay?'

She nodded, swiping her eyes. 'I'm sorry...' she managed, embarrassed. As well as heartsore. She'd spent the last year trying to persuade Adam she was a competent businesswoman, and now she'd trashed that, too.

'Don't apologise,' he said, but then he surprised her even more when he asked, gently, 'Can you tell me what the problem is?'

She nodded again. But she couldn't look at him. 'Cade left me.'

She heard him curse under his breath, a very un-Adam-like expletive.

'And I'm going to have his baby.'

His hand tensed on her shoulder. 'Wait a minute. Landry got you pregnant, then dumped you?' He swore again, sounding furious.

She blinked. How odd. The show of emotion was so un-Adam-like, that and the fact he didn't look exasperated with her.

'To be fair, the getting pregnant bit was a joint enterprise,' she replied.

He shot off the couch and stormed across the thick carpeting, his rigid strides making his agitation clear. She hadn't intended to tell him about the baby, because she didn't think she could cope with a lecture. But all he did was continue to curse about Cade.

'You don't blame me?' she said, still astonished by his reaction as he marched back towards her.

'Blame you for what?'

'For getting pregnant with your business rival?'

His frown became a scowl. 'Do you want the baby?'

She nodded.

'Then blame has nothing to do with it,' he said without hesitation. 'But Landry has responsibilities, to you *and* to his child.' He thrust his fingers through his hair, making it stick up in haphazard spikes. 'I can't believe it...' he said, sitting heavily on the couch next to her. 'I'm going to be an uncle.'

She found herself smiling. It felt good, even though it hurt.

She sniffed. Then blew her nose loudly on the tissue. 'I didn't actually come here to tell you about the baby. It's not due for months,' she said. It felt important to have his support, especially as it was so unexpected, but it didn't really change anything.

'I'm going to kill him,' her brother said, apropos to nothing.

'Adam, really.' She laid her hand on one of the fists clenched in his lap. 'It's okay. He's been very generous. He's insisting on supporting the baby financially.' She'd heard from his team the day after he'd walked out. But somehow his generosity only made the whole thing so much worse. Because she couldn't hate him the way she wanted to be able to hate him.

'That's not the point, Charley,' her brother said, flipping his hand over to grip her fingers—reminding her of the eighteen-year-old who had anchored her once before, when he had been in so much pain himself. 'The point is he hurt you. He made you cry.'

She clasped his hand, fighting off more tears. 'Please don't be nice now, or you'll make me start crying again. And neither of us wants that.' She tried to smile. 'You know what's good about all this, though?'

He simply looked at her blankly.

'It's nice to have my big brother in my corner,' she said.

He folded her back into his arms. 'Of course I'm in your corner. Where the hell else would I be?'

She sighed against his damp shirt. 'I don't know…but let's face it, I haven't always been very lovable,' she said. 'Which is probably why Cade didn't want me either.'

She'd had to face that truth so many times over the last few days as she struggled to make sense of Cade's abrupt departure.

What an idiot she'd been—building up some ridiculous fantasy they could become a family while busy pretending all her flaws didn't exist. Convenient, but not reality. Why would she assume Cade would want her for the long haul when no one else ever had?

She had thought they'd made a connection, but what did she really know about honest, open relationships, seeing as she'd never had one of those either?

'Please tell me he didn't say that to you?' Adam demanded, looking even more furious.

She shook her head. 'Honestly? He didn't really give me an explanation. He told me he wanted this baby. And somehow I made a silly mistake and got that confused with him wanting me too. But while I was falling in love…he wasn't.'

Adam dragged her back, his hands gripping her shoulders as he stared into her face. 'Why the hell would he tell you he wanted the baby if he *didn't* want you too?' he said. 'It doesn't sound like you made a mistake. It sounds like he deliberately misled you. And who the hell wouldn't want you?'

She could feel the tears welling again at his forthright defence of her. If she didn't feel so broken right now, she would have been able to appreciate it more. Then the other things he'd said registered... 'But why would he mislead me about wanting the baby?'

'The bet,' he said, then cursed again.

The bet? She felt sick. The nausea she hadn't felt in weeks dropped into her stomach like a stone.

Was that possible? That Cade had been lying to her about the baby? Simply to ensure she would stay with him for those extra weeks? Could he have done something so manipulative?

'I can't believe he would be that cruel,' she said, desperate not to think it of him. But she'd been wrong about so much else. Why not this too? 'Do you really think he would lie about that?' she asked, feeling more insecure now, and vulnerable.

'Honestly, Charley, I don't know him *that* well,' he said, but she could see the sympathy in his eyes and the understanding. Why did that only make her stomach hurt worse? 'But I do know he's pretty ruthless in business, and he really wanted Helberg.'

'But so did you,' Charley said, still trying to clarify, to reject Adam's accusations. Cade had never told her why owning Helberg was so important to him, but could it really have been *that* important?

'Yeah, I did, because I wanted Montague's for personal reasons which I now know were pretty misguided.'

'What reasons?' she asked. Was it possible that Cade had had really compelling reasons too? Personal reasons? But even if he did, how could that absolve him? And why was she still making excuses for him?

Adam interrupted her panicked justifications. 'I wanted to get it back because I thought I was to blame for Mum's suicide.'

'What?' Charley's heart lurched in her chest at the flash of pain in his expression. 'But...*why* would you think that?'

He sat back down next to her and took her hands in his. 'That's not the point, Charley. The point is I don't think that any more. Ella made me realise her suicide wasn't my fault. Any more than it was *your* fault that both our parents ignored you growing up.'

'Okay,' she said, surprised at his intuition...but also strangely empowered by the bold statement. He was right. A part of her *had* always believed it was her fault. And she supposed she had internalised that hurt, that feeling of rejection. But how did Adam know? Then again, Adam did seem different today. Not just more relaxed and a lot less guarded, but also surprisingly emotionally astute. 'Who's Ella?' she asked, wondering if this woman she had never heard of had something to do with it.

Flags of colour appeared on his cheeks. 'It's a long story...and I'd like you to meet her. *Soon*,' he said forcefully. But before she could get over her shock—was her commitment-phobic brother actually in love?—he squeezed her fingers and added, 'I think we should focus on Cade first. And how exactly we're going to make him pay for this...'

'There is no *we*, Adam.' She tugged her hands out of her brother's grip. And stood up. Her legs were still shaky, her insides twisted into hard, greasy knots. But Adam's support had finally made her realise something important. They had both been failed by their parents. And she'd carried that subconscious belief—that she needed to earn approval and attention, because she didn't deserve it—ever since she was a child. Did that explain why she'd been such a coward this past week, too...? Dissolving into tears and recriminations and blaming herself for Cade's desertion, without ever really wondering why he'd left?

She had let him walk. She hadn't fought. She hadn't even asked for an explanation. Because deep down she'd blamed herself, still believing that she was essentially unlovable. But if he had done what Adam suspected him of doing—said he wanted this baby just to win a bet...she wanted to know so she could start the long slow process of getting over him. Because if he had, he had never been the man she had fallen in love with—not even close. And the only way to do that was to suck up her pride—and her pain—and confront him. Before she lost her nerve.

'This is my life, and I plan to sort it out,' she added, because Adam was still looking at her with sympathy in his eyes. 'On my own.'

She'd been so scared she wouldn't be good enough to be a mother. Scared she couldn't handle it alone. Terrified of coming to rely on Cade. So that when she had fallen in love and he hadn't loved her back, she'd convinced herself—just like she had as a little girl—that it was her fault, her mistake somehow. But she could see now, whatever Cade's motives, she hadn't been wrong to fall for him. She had simply been wrong not to ensure he deserved her love.

To her surprise, instead of arguing with her or doubting her ability to go it alone, Adam simply nodded. 'Okay, Charley,' he said. 'I hope you give him hell,' he finished with a solidarity he had never shown her before.

Whoever you are, Ella, I love you already.

'Don't worry, I will,' she said, feeling stronger now than she had.

As she left Adam's office and called a cab to take her

to Landry Construction's offices uptown, she realised that whatever Cade's motives turned out to be, she would be okay.

The bottom had dropped out of her world. But she wasn't the one running away. Not this time. That would be Cade.

And not only did she deserve answers from him about why he was running, she also deserved to be loved. And no one was going to convince her otherwise...

Not any more.

CHAPTER SIXTEEN

'MR LANDRY? Miss Courtney is here to see you.'

Cade's gaze rose from his laptop, propelled by the surge of emotion at the mention of Charlotte's name.

'Charlotte's here?' he managed, before the woman herself—the woman who had haunted every one of his dreams and all his nightmares for a week, the woman who he'd had to stop himself returning to a hundred times—marched into the space behind his executive assistant, Grady.

'Yes, Mr Landry...' The young man glanced round, only to be mowed down by Charlotte. 'I'm sorry, Miss...'

'Thank you so much, Grady,' she cut the poor kid's protests off at the knees.

Cade stood and came out from behind his desk.

The emotion turned to pride and a powerful sense of relief. The stunned sadness of a week ago was gone. The sadness he'd caused and hadn't been able to forgive himself for.

'Please, Miss...' Grady began.

'It's okay, Grady,' he said, finally managing to find his voice around the tight, painful feeling in his throat. 'Leave us alone and hold all my calls.'

He hadn't meant to hurt her. But he knew he had. It was just one of the things that had tortured him—the guilt as well as the longing.

Grady left the room and closed the door behind him.

Charlotte stopped beside the drawing table, where he had been working late all this week so he wouldn't have to go back to his apartment alone and think about her.

'It's good to see you, Charlotte,' he said. And meant it.

He didn't know why she was here, and he really didn't care. Because he felt like a starving man eating for the first time in days as he devoured the sight of her in tailored pants and a fitted blouse, her silky hair rioting around her face.

She sucked in a breath, her expression a vivid combination of anger and determination.

'I need to know the truth...' she said carefully, but he could see the swirl of sadness in her eyes, alongside the storm of outrage. 'Did you tell me you wanted this baby when we found out I was pregnant simply to keep me with you until Labor Day? To win Helberg?'

What...?' The accusation came so far out of left field, he couldn't make any sense of it.

'I deserve to know...' she said, her voice rising, her face rigid now with hurt. 'Because Adam believes you did, and the way you left... I need to know exactly how much you used me and the baby to win the bet. So I can start to forgive myself for falling in love with you.'

Falling in love with you...

The words made the ache in his throat sink into his heart.

He stared at her, desperately trying to figure out what to say. Part of him knew he should tell her she was right. That he'd never really wanted this baby, that he'd used the pregnancy the same way he'd used her. Wouldn't it be better for all of them? It would be the final nail in the coffin of this relationship. The relationship he'd been so terrified of nurturing or even acknowledging a week ago, when they'd seen the baby for the first time.

But somehow the words which would set him free, which would set them both free, wouldn't come out of his mouth. Because he had missed her, so much, and he still wanted her, and he couldn't bear to lie to her again.

So he continued to stand there dumbly, absorbing the sight of her, unable to say anything at all.

She stepped forward, the sound of her pumps somehow deafening on the office carpeting. The sheen of moisture in her eyes twinkled in the afternoon light pouring through the windows…and everything inside him became harsh and jagged. The intense longing to touch her again, to hold her, to never let her go was like a kudzu vine wrapping around his heart and squeezing hard enough to make his breathing stop.

'I didn't set out to hurt you…' he said at last, which was at least the truth. But how could he have known she would come to mean so much?

'You coward…' she hissed, the single tear running down her cheek like an arrow to his heart. 'You can't admit it even now, can you? Why did you say you wanted the baby? When you didn't? How could you use the pregnancy just to win a bet?'

He should let her believe it, but the pain in her voice broke him.

'Because I didn't. The bet had nothing to do with my feelings for the baby…'

Or you.

She walked forward, lifting her fists, and pushing them against his chest. 'You're lying. I know you're lying.' Her sobs wrenched at his heart. 'Or why would you leave as soon as you won?'

'It wasn't about the bet...' He grasped her fists and tugged her into his arms, no longer able to stop himself from holding her. 'Not even in Italy.'

He felt the anger drain out of her until all that was left was the hurt.

She looked up at him, her ravaged face somehow so brave. 'Then why did you leave me?'

He cupped her cheeks, brushed the last of her tears away with his thumbs. The brutal agony washed through him all over again. That terrible feeling of never being good enough, strong enough, to matter.

But he'd mattered to her. And he'd thrown it away.

'I'm not sure I can explain it,' he said, so glad to have her in his arms again he was scared even now to tell her what a coward he'd been.

She shook her head, then dragged herself back, out of his embrace. He felt the loss like a blow to the chest. She was trembling, the pain in her eyes unvarnished, but despite the hurt he could also see her strength, which only made him love and respect her more.

'That's not good enough, Cade. You made me believe it was my fault, but worse than that, when Adam mentioned the bet...' She drew in a ragged breath. 'I realised I didn't know you well enough to tell if it were true. Because you always kept so much hidden.' She swung away from him and walked to the glass wall, which looked down on the city he'd conquered. Achievements which meant nothing without her. 'And that made me blame myself. Made me think it was my fault somehow...'

'Damn it, Charlotte.' He walked towards her, grasped

her shoulders from behind, and pressed his face into her hair, unable to stop touching her, needing to hold her again. 'You have to believe me,' he said, inhaling the scent which had become a drug over the past weeks. 'I didn't walk away because of the bet.'

She turned to face him, dislodging his hands. And wrapped her arms around her waist to ward him off. 'Still not good enough, Cade. You have to tell me why you left.'

He sighed and drew back. And turned to stare out at the view, not able to look at her when he told her the truth.

They were so far above the manic energy of Manhattan. He should have been safe here, in the ivory tower he'd built to protect himself from ever needing anyone again.

But she'd breached it, just like she'd breached his heart.

'Because I was terrified of my feelings for you,' he murmured. 'Seeing the baby felt so real, but what was worse was knowing that eventually I would let him down. And you down. I had to leave you first, before you decided to leave me, like she did.'

Charley stood shaking, the emotion coursing through her almost more than she could bear. But then slowly, Cade's words registered. The fear behind them, but also the simplicity of feeling, the strength of his longing. Like hers.

But she didn't want to give in too easily. To be that needy girl again who had internalised all the hurt, the longing, the loneliness of her childhood. Now more than ever, she needed to be strong. She wasn't going to give him a free pass. If he loved her, *really* loved her, he had to prove it to her. She deserved that.

'But then why did you still close the deal?' she asked,

her voice thick with tears. 'If you wanted to be with me? If you were simply scared of your feelings for me...' She let out a heavy sigh. 'Which I get, because frankly, I was pretty terrified of my feelings for you,' she added. He finally turned to look at her again, the shame in his expression giving her the strength she needed to say the rest of it. 'Why did you still claim Helberg?'

He dropped his head, shoved his hands into the pockets of his trousers, his stance so tense she could see what it was costing him to find words for feelings she doubted he had ever confronted before.

He lifted his head at last, his blue eyes dark with the emotion he'd refused to let her see...until now.

'I thought if I claimed Helberg,' he said, his words measured, but the tone brittle with self-loathing, 'I could get back the feeling of being safe again. Of being invulnerable.' He shook his head. 'But it didn't make any difference. Even though I've been working to acquire the damn brand for...' He sighed and looked down at his feet again. 'A long time.'

'Why?' she asked, because she wanted all the answers to questions she'd never felt able to ask him before. '*Why* was Helberg so important to you?'

He raised his head, the scar on his eyebrow levelling as he frowned. But just when she thought he wasn't going to tell her, he let out a rough, guttural, hopeless sigh.

'It's pretty dumb,' he said.

'Not to me it isn't.' She wouldn't let him off the hook.

He looked away, but when he began to talk, she knew the monotone of his voice masked a deep emotion she doubted he had ever revealed to anyone before now.

'The department store…in Baton Rouge,' he said, but then his voice trailed off.

'The place where your mother abandoned you?' she prompted.

His gaze met hers. And he nodded. 'It was Helberg's flagship store in the South. She used to take me there when she wasn't too strung out. She knew I liked to play in the toy department. And the staff were kind. They'd let us stay for hours and never threw us out.' He hitched his shoulder, the gesture somehow both wary and ashamed. 'I loved that place so much. It was clean, and everything was perfect. It's the only good memory I have of her. She wasn't much of a mama, but she was so young and messed up. I think, deep down, I figured if I could own Helberg, restore the brand, bring it back to its former glory, I could prove she had loved me once, too.'

She stood trembling. The picture he'd painted was so sad and so vulnerable. And she realised however much he had tried to leave that boy behind, that abandoned child had always been there inside him. Scared to love. Terrified to ask for more. In case it made him that vulnerable again.

No wonder he had been frightened of the love building between them, too.

She walked to him, banded her arms around his waist and pressed her cheek to the rigid muscles of his chest. 'Oh, Cade, you idiot.'

He wrapped her in his arms, the deep sigh making his muscles relax. 'Can you forgive me for being such a dumbass?'

He shifted back, framed her face in his palms, then pressed his forehead to hers. 'If you'll give me another chance, I swear I can make it up to you,' he vowed. 'Every damn day. I love you, Charlotte, so damn much. I'm gonna sell Helberg. It never meant what I thought it did anyway.'

The hope blossomed inside her, stronger this time. And so much more sure.

'I don't want you to do that, Cade. Especially if Helberg is your only real connection to your mother.'

He gave her a weak smile, but she could see the same fierce hope reflected in his eyes.

'Don't you get it, Charlotte? I don't need Helberg now.' He boosted her into his arms, the smile becoming a grin as she stroked his hair, his cheeks, the rough stubble on his chin, letting him know they were good. They were okay again. That she had already forgiven him. 'Not if I've got you. And our baby.'

She chuckled, elated, as he captured her face and began to kiss her as if his life depended on sealing their connection, exploiting it. And glorying in it.

And as he showed her how much he loved her, she knew exactly how he felt.

Because her life depended on it, too.

EPILOGUE

One year later

'DO THEY FUSS like that a lot?'

Cade smiled at the question from Zane deMarco as he stood in the bright, airy kitchen of his new home—a historic brownstone with a big yard and ten bedrooms he'd bought seven months ago—and tried to soothe his fretful son. Luke Adam Landry was not happy at having been detached from his mama's breast five minutes ago—despite being fast asleep—and he was letting Cade and Zane and his uncle Adam know all about it.

'Only at three in the morning, usually,' Cade joked.

Zane's eyebrows lifted, but he looked more fascinated than horrified when he said, 'Seriously?'

Yeah, seriously, and at two and five and any time in between.

'Not always,' he said, deciding to give Zane a break.

Their small party had found out at the neighbourhood chapel only an hour ago, while they were baptising Luke, and Zane and Adam had been sworn in as his godfathers, that Zane and his partner, Skylar, were expecting. Seemed it had been a surprise for both of them, but a happy surprise, and Cade didn't want to scare the guy too much. Especially as all the trials and tribulations of parenthood in the past three months had been far outweighed, in Cade's humble opinion, by the incredible upside of meeting his son. And watching Charlotte blossom into the role of motherhood. She was magnificent, and he could not have loved her more if he had tried.

'He's just a little mad with me at the moment for interrupting his quality time with his mama,' he said easily—and just like his mama, Luke was more than ready to let anyone and everyone know his mind, Cade thought, his chest swelling with pride. 'And for letting the preacher dunk him in water. I'm not sure he's gonna forgive me for that for a while,' he added, remembering the indignant yelling in church which had nearly deafened them all.

Adam gave his new nephew a pat on the back. 'Good boy, Luke. You tell your daddy when he's out of order, and I'll back you up.'

All three of them laughed, but as Luke finally quietened, nestling against Cade's chest and dropping back to sleep with his whole fist shoved into his mouth, Cade remembered something he and Charlotte had agreed to that morning. 'By the way, Courtney, I have a baptismal gift for you.'

Adam's expression sobered. 'A gift? For me? But I'm not the one getting christened,' he said.

Trust the guy to be so damn literal.

But Cade only smiled. He liked Adam Courtney, a lot. All three of them had become much more than just squash buddies over the past year.

Although he found it hilarious now to think of them sat in their club sauna—the club they rarely had time to go to now—making that dumb bet to decide who would own

Helberg Holdings, only to all end up winning something much more precious instead.

He liked Zane and Adam's partners too—Skylar and Ella—who he and Charlotte socialised with now whenever all six of them were in the city.

'Charlotte and I would like to give you Montague's,' he said, cutting straight to the chase.

The work to rebuild the Helberg brand in the past year ever since the buyout had kept him busy—while he waited for Charlotte to pop and they'd both got to know their new son. But he had decided to offload Montague's and a few of the other assets. He'd wanted to gift the company to Charlotte, when he'd found out the connection to her mother, but she had insisted he give it to her brother instead. And he hadn't had a problem with that.

'Thanks,' Adam said easily. 'But I don't need it.'

'I'd really like you to take it, man,' Cade countered. 'Both Charlotte and I owe you—and Ella—big time for supporting us this past year.'

And helping give Charlotte the courage to realise our break-up was all my fault, not hers, he almost added, but didn't. Because as much as he liked and admired his new brother-in-law, and considered him a good friend, they were still guys.

'And she wants you to have it. She's far too busy with Trouble Maker...' His chest swelled again at the thought of how Charlotte had developed her business over the past year, mostly while pregnant. 'And with this little fella...' He kissed his son's downy curls, breathing in the sweet scent he adored of sour milk and baby shampoo. 'So she doesn't have the time to give Montague's the attention it needs.'

Adam looked non-plussed. 'Okay, how about I think about it?'

'You do that,' Cade nodded, realising how important it was to him to pay his dues to Adam Courtney… Because the man was part of Cade's family now too.

'Glad you two got that settled,' Zane cut in, the reckless twinkle in his eye something Cade remembered from a certain sauna meeting on last year's Independence Day. 'Now where the hell is my gift? Because I've got my eye on some prime realty in SoHo that belongs to Landry Construction.'

'Go to hell,' Cade joked back, and they all laughed.

Four hours later…

'He's finally back to sleep. I swear he is almost as much of a handful as you are.'

'That's my boy!' Charley grinned at Cade in the bathroom mirror and popped her toothbrush onto its stand, unable to disguise her happiness at his exasperation…and the mouth-watering sight of his naked chest, the phoenix tattoo she adored highlighting his impressive pecs.

It was only ten o'clock, but they'd had a very full day, getting their son formally baptised and then enjoying some quality time with Adam and Ella and Zane and Skylar. She was more than ready for bed now. Especially when Cade wrapped his arms around her waist from behind and pulled her against him.

'I think I should punish you for encouraging him to defy me,' he murmured into her hair, his hands rising to cup and caress her breasts through the silk negligée she had worn specifically to get this reaction.

Excitement swirled alongside the joy as she felt the ridge

growing in his pyjama pants to press against her bottom. They'd finally restarted their love life a month ago, and to her utter joy, it was as vital and exciting as ever…although they had to snatch their chances when they could now, because Cade wasn't wrong—Luke was somewhat demanding.

Although she wouldn't have had it any other way.

She lifted her arm to curl her hand around his neck, her mind floating on the delicious wave of arousal and all the happy memories.

So much had happened in the past year, all of it full-on and chaotic and challenging and exhausting.

They'd got married in a small ceremony in Baton Rouge just before Christmas, to coincide with the opening of the new Landry Helberg Department Store—with Adam giving her away and Ella, who Charley already considered a sister, as her maid of honour. She'd also expanded the Trouble Maker brand into a fashion line, and recently moved to new premises in the brownstone next door—which Cade had purchased for her as a wedding present, and then gutted and rehabbed into an amazing shop and workspace. She'd had to take a back seat on her business, though, once Luke was born, but taking the time to nurture and enjoy her son had been more than worth it. The fear she'd once had of being a mother had been well and truly conquered by the rush of pure, unadulterated love she felt for their baby the minute he had been placed in her arms, protesting about the ten hours of labour he had just endured.

What had surprised her much more, though, was how willing Cade had been to reduce his workload too. And spend as much time as he could being a hands-on dad.

'Mmm…' she purred as Cade's questing fingers lifted

her negligée to find her wet and ready for him. 'I think maybe we need to take my punishment into the bedroom,' she said, making him chuckle.

She swung round and leapt into his arms. And he caught her. Of course.

She shouldn't be surprised, she realised as she peppered kisses over his handsome face, that Cade had become such a hands-on dad. Because he had been as good as his word over the past year in every respect. More than ready to prove how much both she and now Luke meant to him.

'Do your worst, Mr Landry!' she announced as he marched into their bedroom.

'Count on it, Mrs Landry,' he said, then threw her on the bed…and proceeded to punish her in the most delicious way possible.

* * * * *

Did you fall head over heels for
After-Party Consequences?

Then you're sure to adore the other
installments in the Billion-Dollar Bet trilogy:
Billion-Dollar Dating Game *by Natalie Anderson*
Boss with Benefits *by Lucy King*

And don't miss these other Heidi Rice stories!

Stolen for His Desert Throne
Redeemed by My Forbidden Housekeeper
Undoing His Innocent Enemy
Hidden Heir with His Housekeeper
Revenge in Paradise

Available now!